Enid Bl

THE WITCH'S CAT

and other stories about cats

Illustrated by
Paul Crompton
and Joyce Johnson

World International Publishing Limited
Manchester

Published in Great Britain by World International
Publishing Limited,
An Egmont Company, Egmont House, PO Box 111,
Great Ducie Street,
Manchester M60 3BL.
Printed in Italy.

British Library Cataloguing in Publication Data
Blyton, Enid 1897–1968
The witch's cat and other stories about cats.
I. Title II. Series
823.912 [J]

ISBN 0–7498–0301–0

Cover illustration by Robin Lawrie

Contents

Enid Blyton

Enid Blyton was born in London in 1897. Her childhood was spent in Beckenham, Kent, and as a child she began to write poems, stories and plays. She trained to be a teacher but she devoted her whole life to being a children's author. Her first book was a collection of poems for children, published in 1922. In 1926 she began to write a weekly magazine for children called *Sunny Stories*, and it was here that many of her most popular stories and characters first appeared. The magazine was immensely popular and in 1953 it became *The Enid Blyton Magazine*.

She wrote more than 600 books for children and many of her most popular series are still published all over the world. Her books have been translated into over 30 languages. Enid Blyton died in 1968.

The witch's cat

Old Dame Kirri was a witch. You could tell she was because she had bright green eyes. She was a good witch though, and spent most of her time making good spells to help people who were ill or unhappy.

She lived in Toppling Cottage, which was just like its name, and looked exactly as if it was going to topple over. But it was kept up by strong magic, and not a brick had fallen, although the cottage was five hundred years old.

At the back of the cottage was the witch's garden. Round it ran a very, very high wall, taller than the tallest man.

"I like a high wall. It keeps people

from peeping and prying," said old Witch Kirri. "In my garden I grow a lot of strange and powerful herbs. I don't want people to see them and steal them. I won't have people making spells from my magic herbs – they might make bad ones."

The witch had a cat. It was black and big, and had green eyes very like the witch's. Its name was Cinder-Boy.

Cinder-Boy helped the witch with her spells. He was really a remarkably clever cat. He knew how to sit exactly in the middle of a chalk ring without moving, whilst Kirri the witch danced round and sang spells. He knew how to go out and collect dew-drops in the moonlight. He took a special little silver cup for that, and never spilt a drop.

He never drank milk. He liked tea, made as strong as the witch made for herself. Sometimes he would sit and sip his tea and purr, and the witch would sip *her* tea and purr, too. It was funny to see them.

Cinder-Boy loved to sleep in the walled-in garden. He knew all the flowers and herbs there. No weeds were allowed to grow. Cinder-Boy scratched them all up.

But one day he came to a small plant growing at the foot of the wall. It had leaves like a rose-tree. It had pale pink flowers, with a mass of yellow stamens in the middle. It smelt very sweet.

"What flower are you?" said Cinder-Boy. "You smell rather like a rose."

"Well, that's just what I am," said the plant. "I'm a wild rose."

"How did you get here?" said Cinder-Boy, surprised.

"A bird dropped a seed," said the wild rose. "But I don't like being here, black cat."

"My name is Cinder-Boy," said the witch's cat. "Why don't you like being here? It is a very nice place to be."

"Well, I feel shut in," said the wild rose. "I'm not very large. If I was taller than the wall I could grow up into the air, and see over the top. I don't like being down here at the bottom, shut in."

"Well, grow tall then," said Cinder-Boy. "I can give you a spell to make your stems nice and long, if you like. Then you can reach up to the top of the wall and look over. There's a nice view there, I can tell you."

"Oh, would you do that?" said the wild rose in delight. "Thank you!"

So Cinder-Boy went off to get a spell to make the stems of the wild rose grow very long. He soon found one. It was in a small blue bottle, and he poured it into a watering-can. The spell was blue, too.

Then he watered the wild rose with the spell, and it began to work almost at once. In two or three days the stems of the wild rose plant had grown quite high into the air.

"Go on growing. You will soon be at the top of the wall!" said Cinder-Boy. So the wild rose went on making its stems longer and longer, hoping to get to the very top of the wall.

But when Cinder-Boy next strolled out into the garden to see how it was getting on, what a shock he had! Every single stem was bent over and lay sprawling over the grass!

"Why, what has happened?" said Cinder-Boy, waving his tail in surprise.

"My stalks grew tall, but they didn't grow strong," said the wild rose, sadly. "Just as I reached the top of the wall, they all flopped over and fell down. They are not strong enough to bear their own weight."

"Well, how do plants with weak stems manage to climb high then?" said Cinder-Boy, puzzled. "Runner beans grow high and they have very weak stems. Sweet peas grow high, and they have weak stems too. I'll go and see how they do it."

So off he went, for the witch grew both in the garden. He soon came back.

"The beans twine their stalks around poles," he said, "and the sweet peas grow little green fingers, called tendrils, which catch hold of things, and they pull themselves up high like that. Can't you do that?"

The wild rose couldn't. It didn't know how to. Its stems wouldn't twist themselves, however much it tried to make them do so. And it couldn't grow a tendril at all.

"Well, we must think of another way," said the cat.

"Cinder-Boy, how do *you* get up to the top of the wall?" asked the wild rose. "You are often up there in the sun. I see you. Well, how do *you* get to the top?"

"I run up the trees," said Cinder-Boy. "Do you see the young fruit trees near you? Well, I run up those to the top of the wall. I use my claws to help me. I dig them into the bark of the trees, and hold on with them."

He showed the wild rose his big curved claws. "I can put them in or out as I like," he said. "They are very useful claws."

The wild rose thought they were too. "If I grew claws like that I could easily climb up the fruit trees, right through them to the top, and then I'd be waving at the top of the wall," it said. "Can't you get me some claws like yours, Cinder-Boy?"

The cat blinked his green eyes and thought hard. "I know what I could do," he said. "I could ask the witch Kirri, my mistress, to make some magic claws that would grow on you. I'll ask her today. In return you must promise to grow her some lovely scarlet hip berries that she can trim her hats and bonnets with in the autumn."

"Oh, I will, I will," promised the wild rose. So Cinder-Boy went off to the witch Kirri and asked her for what he wanted.

She grumbled a little. "It is difficult to make claws," she said. "Very difficult. You will have to help me, Cinder-Boy. You will have to sit in the middle of a blue ring of chalk, and put out all your claws at once, whilst I sing a magic song. Don't be scared at what happens."

Cinder-Boy went to sit in the middle of a chalk ring that the witch drew in the middle of the garden. He stuck out all his claws as she commanded.

She danced round with her broomstick, singing such a magic song that Cinder-Boy felt quite scared. Then a funny thing happened.

His claws fell out on to the ground with a clatter – and they turned red or green as they fell. He looked at his paws and saw new ones growing. Then those fell out, too. How very, very strange!

Soon there was quite a pile of claws on the ground. Then the witch stopped singing and dancing, and rubbed out the ring of chalk.

"You can come out now, Cinder-Boy," she said. "The magic is finished."

Cinder-Boy collected all the red and green claws. They were strong and curved and sharp. He took them to the bottom of the garden, and came to the wild rose.

"I've got claws for you!" he said. "The witch Kirri did some strong magic. Look, here they are. I'll press each one into your stems, till you have claws all down them. Then I'll say a growing spell, and they will grow into you properly, and belong to you."

So Cinder-Boy did that, and the wild

rose felt the cat-claws growing firmly into the long stems.

"Now," said Cinder-Boy, in excitement, "now you will be able to climb up through the fruit tree, wild rose. I will help you at first."

So Cinder-Boy took the wild rose stems, all set with claws, and pushed them up into the little fruit tree that grew near by. The claws took hold of the bark and held on firmly. Soon all the stems were climbing up high through the little fruit tree, the claws digging themselves into the trunk and the branches.

The wild rose grew higher. It pulled itself up by its new claws. It was soon at the top of the wall! It could see right over it to the big world beyond.

"Now I'm happy!" said the wild rose to Cinder-Boy. "Come and sit up here on the wall beside me. Let us look at the big world together. Oh, Cinder-Boy, it is lovely up here. I am not shut in any longer. Thank you for my claws.

I do hope I shall go on growing them now."

It did. And it grew beautiful scarlet berries in the autumn, for witch Kirri's winter bonnets. You should see how pretty they are when she trims them with the rose hips!

Ever since that day the wild roses have grown cats' claws all down their stems, sometimes green and sometimes red or pink. They use them to climb with. Have you seen them? If you haven't, do go and look. It will surprise you to see cats' claws growing out of a plant!

It was a good idea of Cinder-Boy's, wasn't it?

The clever kitten

Cosy was a little tabby kitten, five months old. She was called Cosy because she always looked such a cosy bundle when she curled herself up on a cushion.

She lived upstairs in the playroom, and the children made a great fuss of her. But Mummy said she must soon be a kitchen cat and go and catch mice in the larder.

The children were upset. They did so love having Cosy in the playroom. Sometimes she slept in the doll's cot, and often she went out for a walk wheeled in the doll's pram.

"Mummy! If you make her live in the kitchen she will grow fat and lazy and

won't play any more!" said Lucy. "Oh, please, do let her belong to us and be the playroom cat."

But their mother didn't seem to think it would be a good idea at all. So Cosy was told that for one week more she could be a playroom kitten – and then she must go downstairs and become a kitchen cat.

Now, one afternoon Cosy had a shock. She was sitting upstairs in the armchair, dozing, wondering if she should get up and try and catch a fly that was buzzing round the table when she suddenly saw somebody looking right in through the window.

Cosy jumped and spat. She arched her little striped back and hissed at the face that looked in at the window. She knew who it was. It was the garden-boy, Alfred, who had sometimes caught her and pulled her tail. And now here was Alfred staring in at the playroom window. Whatever was he there for?

The playroom was upstairs. Cosy wondered if Alfred had suddenly grown legs long enough to reach to the nursery. It was most extraordinary. She didn't know that Alfred was standing on a ladder. He had been sent up to tie a big branch of the climbing rose-tree that had got loose.

Alfred stared into the playroom. The cupboard door was open, and in the cupboard Alfred saw things that made his mouth water. There was a bag of sugar lumps. A tin of biscuits stood there too. A bottle of sweets was next to it. A bar of chocolate was near by. Goodness! Alfred thought it was marvellous to see so many good things together.

He looked down into the garden. Nobody was there. He peered carefully into the playroom. Nobody was there either.

"I'll chance it!" said Alfred to himself. "I could get all those things into my pocket!"

Now as Alfred climbed in at the window, he pushed the ladder, quite by accident, and it fell to the ground below! And there was Alfred in the playroom, with no ladder to get down again by! He would have to go down the stairs.

Cosy the kitten glared at him. She didn't like the unkind garden-boy at all. She spat and hissed at him. He threw a brick at her from the brick box and it hit Cosy on the tail. The kitten leapt out of the chair and flew at Alfred. She scratched him on his hand. Oh, if only,

only she could make someone come and catch this bad boy before he took all the things out of the cupboard!

And then Cosy had a marvellous idea! The playroom piano lid was open. She had often seen Lucy playing on it, making all kinds of noises, deep and loud, and high and tinkly. Perhaps Cosy could make a noise on it too, and then someone might hear and come to the playroom!

So Cosy leapt up on to the open piano and ran up and down the black and

white keys. "Ping, ping, pong, dingle, dingle, doom!" went the keys, making a funny little tune of their own.

Cosy was rather frightened. It was funny to make noises with her feet. But she went on and on running up and down the piano, though Alfred threw another brick at her to make her get off!

Now Mummy was sitting in the room below, reading. She knew that the children were out. And when she heard the strange noise going on upstairs she couldn't *imagine* what it was!

She jumped up and listened. "Ping, ping, pong, dingle, dingle, DOOM!" went the noise. The loud, deep DOOM sound was the lowest key on the piano.

"It's someone banging about on the playroom piano!" said Mummy, in great astonishment. "Whoever can it be?"

She ran upstairs to see – and when she got to the playroom, what did she find but Alfred stuffing his pockets full of sugar lumps and sweets and biscuits! And there was Cosy still on the piano, playing the keys by running up and down, up and down!

"ALFRED!" said Mummy. And how Alfred jumped! In two minutes he was downstairs, and the gardener was telling him just exactly what he thought of him, and just what happened to bad boys who climbed in at other people's windows and stole. What a shock for Alfred!

But how thrilled the children were when they came home and heard all that had happened!

"Clever little Cosy!" cried Lucy, picking up the purring kitten. "Mummy, don't make her into a kitchen cat, please, please, don't! Why, she can even play the playroom piano! And she has saved all our biscuits and sweets and sugar. Do let her belong to the playroom always and always!"

"Very well," said Mummy, with a laugh. "You can have Cosy for your own. But do teach her to play the piano properly, because although the noise she made was very good for catching a thief, I wouldn't at all like to hear it going on all day long!"

So Lucy is going to teach Cosy to play the piano properly. Do you think she will be able to?

The cat without whiskers

Inky was a black cat, with the finest white whiskers in the street. He was a handsome cat, with sharp ears and a long thick tail that looked like a snake when he waved it to and fro. He had a white mark under his chin which the children called his feeder, and he washed it three times a day, so that it was always like snow.

Inky was plump, for he was the best ratter and mouser in the town, and never lacked a good dinner. When he sat on the wall washing himself he was a fine sight, for his glossy fur gleamed in the sun and his whiskers stuck out each side of his face like white wires.

"I'm the finest-looking cat in the

town," said Inky proudly, and he looked scornfully down at the tabby in the garden below, and the white cat washing itself on a window-sill near by. "Nobody is as good-looking as me!"

Then there came by a little boy, and when he saw the big black cat sitting up on the wall, he shouted up at him, laughing, "Hallo, Whiskers!"

Inky was offended. His name wasn't Whiskers. It was Inky. A little girl heard what the boy said and she laughed. "That's a good name for him," she said. "He's a very whiskery cat. Whiskers! Whiskers!"

Everyone thought it a funny name, and soon Inky was being called Whiskers all day long, even by the cats and dogs around. This made him really very angry.

"It's a horrid, silly name," he thought crossly, "and it's rude of people to call me that. They don't call that nice old gentleman with the beard 'Whiskers',

do they? And they don't shout 'Nosy' at that boy with the big nose. I shan't answer them when they call me Whiskers!"

So he didn't – but it wasn't any good, for everyone shouted "Whiskers! Whiskers!" as soon as they saw Inky's wonderful whiskers.

Inky thought hard. "I shall get rid of my whiskers," he said to himself. "Yes

– I shall start a new fashion for cats. We won't have whiskers. After all, men shave every morning, and people think that is a good idea. I will shave my whiskers off, and then no one will call me Whiskers."

He told his idea to wise old Shellyback the tortoise. Shellyback listened and pulled at the grass he was eating.

"It is best not to meddle with things you have been given," he said. "You will be sorry."

"No, I shan't," said Inky. "My whiskers are no use to me that I can see – I shall shave them off!"

Well, he slipped into the bathroom at his home early the next morning and found the thing his master called a razor. In a trice Inky had shaved his beautiful whiskers off. They were gone. He was no longer a whiskery cat.

He looked at himself in the glass. He did look a bit strange – but at any rate no one would now shout Whiskers after him. He slipped down the stairs and out into the garden. He jumped on the wall in the sun.

The milkman came by and looked at him. He did not shout "Whiskers!" as he usually did. He stared in rather a puzzled way and said nothing at all. Then a little boy came by delivering papers, and he didn't shout "Whiskers!" either.

Inky was pleased. At last he had got rid of his horrid name. He sat in the sun, purring, and soon his friends gathered round him. There was Tabby from next door, the white cat Snowball, Shellyback the tortoise, who looked up at him from the lawn, and the old dog Rover, who never chased cats.

"What's the matter with you this morning, Inky?" asked Snowball, puzzled. "You look different."

"His whiskers are gone," said Tabby, startled. "How strange."

"How did you lose them?" asked Rover.

"I shaved them off," said Inky

proudly. "I am starting a new fashion for cats. Grown-up men shave their whiskers off each day, don't they? Well, why should cats have whiskers? Don't you think I look much smarter now?"

Everyone stared at Inky, but nobody said a word. They all thought Inky looked dreadful without his whiskers.

"You'll soon see every animal following my fashion of no whiskers," said Inky. "It's so much more comfortable. Whiskers always get in my way when I'm washing my face, but now I can wash it as smoothly as anything. Look!"

He washed his face with his paw. Certainly it looked easier to do it without whiskers. But the older animals shook their heads.

"Whiskers are some use or we wouldn't have them," said Tabby.

"Well, what use *are* they?" said Inky.

But nobody was clever enough to think of anything to say in answer to that. One by one they slipped off to their homes to dinner, quite determined that *they* were not going to shave off their whiskers, whatever Inky did.

Now that night Inky felt very hungry. He had been late for tea that afternoon and a stray dog had gone into his garden and eaten up the plate of fish and milk that his mistress had put out for him. Inky was annoyed.

"Never mind," he thought to himself. "I'll go hunting tonight. I'll catch a few mice and perhaps a rat or two. I know a good place in the hedge at the bottom of the garden. I'll hide on one side of it and wait for the night animals to come out."

So off he went when darkness came and crouched down on one side of the hedge. Soon he heard the pitter-pattering of little mice-feet. Inky stiffened and kept quite still. In a moment he would squeeze through the hedge and pounce on those foolish mice.

He took a step forward. His paw was like velvet and made no noise. He pushed his head into a hole in the hedge – then his body – but alas for Inky! His body was too big for the hole, and the hedge creaked as he tried to get through. The mice heard the noise and shot off into their holes. Not one was left.

"Bother!" said Inky crossly. "I'll wait again. I believe that old rat has a run here somewhere. I'd like to catch him!"

So he waited – and sure enough the big rat ran silently by the hedge. Inky heard him and began to creep towards him; but his fat body brushed against some leaves and the rat heard and fled.

Inky was astonished. Usually he could hunt marvellously without making a single sound. Why was it that his body seemed so clumsy tonight? Why did he brush against things and make rustling noises? It was most annoying.

And then suddenly he knew the reason why. Although he hadn't thought about it, his fine whiskers had always helped him to hunt. They had stretched out each side of his face, and were just about the width of his body. He had known that if he could get his head and whiskers through a hole without touching anything, his body would go through easily too, without a sound.

"It was my whiskers that helped my

body to know if it could go easily and silently through the holes and between leaves," thought Inky in despair. "Of course! Why didn't I think of that before? They were just the right width for my body, and I knew quite well if I touched anything with my whiskers that my body would also touch it and make a noise – and so I would go another way!"

Inky was quite right. His whiskers had helped him in his hunting. Now he would not be able to hunt well, for he would never know if his body could squeeze through gaps and holes. He would always be making rustling, crackling noises with leaves and twigs. He would never catch anything. Poor Inky!

You can guess that Inky was always waiting for his mistress to put out his dinner after that – for he hardly ever caught a mouse or rat now. He grew much thinner, and he hid himself away, for he was ashamed to think that he had shaved off the things that had been so useful to him.

"A new fashion indeed!" thought Inky. "I was mad! If only I had my lovely whiskers again I wouldn't mind being called "Whiskers" a hundred times a day. My life is spoilt. I shall never be able to hunt again."

He was a sad and unhappy cat, ashamed to talk to anyone except wise old Shellyback the tortoise. One day he told Shellyback why he was unhappy. Shellyback looked at him closely and laughed.

"Go and sit up on the wall in the sun and see what happens," he said to Inky. "You'll find your troubles are not so big as you thought they were."

In surprise Inky jumped up on the wall and sat there in the sun. The milkman came by with his cart. He looked up.

"Hallo, Whiskers!" he shouted. "Good old Whiskers!"

Inky nearly fell off the wall in astonishment. What! He was called Whiskers again even if he had shaved them off? But silly old Inky had quite forgotten something. What had he forgotten?

He had forgotten that whiskers grow again like hair. His whiskers had grown out fine and long and strong and white – and he had been so miserable that he hadn't even noticed. Silly old Whiskers!

He *was* happy when he found that he had them again. He sat and purred so loudly that Shellyback really thought there was an aeroplane flying somewhere near! It sounded just like it.

And now Inky can hunt again, and is the best mouser in the town. He has grown plump and handsome, and his whiskers are finer than ever. He loves to hear himself called "Whiskers" now. So if you see him up on the wall, black and shining, don't say "Hallo, Inky!" – shout "Good old Whiskers!" and he'll purr like a kettle on the boil!

Poor Granny!

When Granny was asleep one day,
My little kitten went to play.
Her ball of knitting wool he found
And chased it round – and round
– and round!
When Granny woke – well, I declare,
She couldn't get up from her chair!

The clever little cat

John and Shirley had a little cat. They had had him since he was a kitten, and they called him Zebby, because he was striped like a zebra.

Zebby was a clever little thing. He hadn't grown very big, but he was strong and healthy. He mewed with joy whenever he saw John and Shirley, for they loved him and were kind to him.

They taught Zebby quite a lot of tricks. The little cat could rattle the handle of a door by standing on his hind legs. He could play hide-and-seek with the children. He could sit up and beg just like a dog.

He rubbed himself against the

children's legs, and purred when he sat on their knees.

"He sounds like the mowing machine!" said Shirley, tickling Zebby round the ears to make him purr more loudly.

But Mummy wasn't quite so pleased with Zebby. "He's a little thief!" she said. "If the food cupboard door is left open he creeps inside and takes whatever he can! And he makes such a noise at night, too, if he's left out. He won't come in when he's called – so he has to be left out – and then he yowls the place down!"

"Oh, Mummy! Zebby's a darling!" said John, and picked up the purring little cat.

"Well, darling or not, Zebby will have to go to another home if he doesn't stop stealing!" said Mummy.

"Do you hear that, Zebby?" asked Shirley. "You must stop at once, because we couldn't bear to lose you. Come and play ball with us."

Zebby ran across the grass with John and Shirley. He was very good with a ball. Whenever he found one he rolled it along with his paw, pretended it was a mouse, jumped at it, sidled all round it, and then set it rolling again. There was nothing he loved quite so much as a ball.

For two days Zebby was very good. Then Mummy and Daddy were going to have a tennis-party, and Mummy bought some salmon to make sandwiches – and, will you believe it, Zebby smelt out that salmon, watched till the food cupboard door was open, and walked in! He hid under the shelf when he heard Cook coming, but as soon as she was out of the way, Zebby jumped up on the shelf and began to eat that nice pink salmon!

So, when Cook went to fetch it for the sandwiches, there was no salmon to be seen, except a bone on the plate, licked quite bare!

"That cat again!" cried Cook, and went to tell Mummy, who was changing into her tennis things. She was very angry.

"You'll have to open the potted meat, Cook," she said. "The bad little cat! I won't keep him in the house a week longer!"

She hunted for Zebby to tell him off, but the little cat had run away to hide. Zebby knew quite well he had done wrong, and he wanted to find somewhere safe.

He ran upstairs. He went into the loft. He jumped out of the loft window on to the roof, and found a nice warm place by the chimney. He curled himself up and went to sleep. Nobody would find him there!

Cook made some potted meat sandwiches. Mummy and Daddy went out to put up the net, and the children tipped out nine new balls on to the green lawn. The guests began to arrive.

John and Shirley were ball-boys. They hunted for the balls that ran into the bushes or bounced over the net into the long orchard grass. They talked about naughty little Zebby.

"I do wish Mummy would let us keep Zebby," said Shirley. "He's been ours for three years now, and he's the nicest little cat I know."

"I wonder where he is," said John. "He's very clever at hiding himself when he's naughty!"

They soon knew where he was! One of the guests hit a ball very wildly and it went spinning up, up, up to the roof of the house! It fell right on Zebby, who was asleep by the chimney, and he woke with a loud squeak of fright. The ball dropped down the roof to the gutter and stayed there.

"There's Zebby!" said Shirley. "Up on the roof! That ball must have woken him up! Zebby, Zebby, Zebby! Come on down!"

But Zebby didn't. He lay there sleepily watching the tennis. Soon another ball flew up on the roof and stuck in the gutter. Zebby watched it with much interest. He got up and strolled down the sloping roof to the gutter.

Mummy was sorry that the balls had gone there because nobody could get them, and they would go rotten in the next rainstorm. But Zebby began to play with the two balls, trying to get them out of the wet gutter.

One ball came out and dropped down to the ground with a big bounce. The children gave a shriek of delight. "Mummy, Zebby's getting the balls off the roof for you!"

Zebby scooped out the second one, but before he could play with it, it dropped to the ground, of course! Everybody laughed and cheered.

"Two good balls saved!" said Daddy. "Thank you, Zebby!"

Zebby waited up on the roof for more balls. Soon one came – and then another – for the court was really too near the house, and many a time balls had been lost in the gutters. Zebby waited for the balls, and wherever they happened to stick he ran to them, and pawed them until he got them free. Then down they fell to the ground.

"What a clever little cat!" cried all the guests. "You must be proud of him! How useful he will be at tennis-parties, too – you will never lose balls in the gutter again!"

Well, Mummy and Daddy did begin to feel very proud of Zebby!

"He's saved no end of new balls for us today," said Daddy. "Can't we keep the food cupboard door shut, Mummy, and keep Zebby?"

"I really think we'd better try," said Mummy – and how John and Shirley cheered! So a spring was fixed to the food cupboard door, and whenever it was left open by mistake the door closed itself – so Zebby could never get inside to steal again.

He's still living with John and Shirley, and when I go there to play tennis I love to see him sitting on the roof waiting

for the balls. Sometimes we send one up there just for fun – we do love to see him paw it out of the gutter and send it down to the ground once more! Isn't he clever?

The cat who flew away

There was once a cat who couldn't be trusted. His name was Whiskers, because he had such fine strong whiskers growing out at each side of his face.

He stole anything and everything he could. He jumped on to the kitchen table directly the cook's back was turned, and jumped off again with a tart, or a kipper, or a sausage in his mouth. Then out of the window he sprang like a flash, before Cook had time to see what he had got.

Whiskers didn't mind what he ate. He was always hungry, and he enjoyed bits of sugar, currants, bread, lemonade, tea leaves, and anything else you can think of that can be found lying on the kitchen table. Nothing seemed to cure him of his wicked ways, and he was so clever that he was hardly ever caught.

Then one day he ate something that gave him a very funny feeling. He didn't know what it was, but he licked it up till it was all gone. Cook had been making cakes, and she had left the self-raising flour on the table. She had gone to change her dress, and there was nobody in the kitchen when Whiskers found the open bag, and began to lick up the flour. It went up his nose and made him sneeze, but he didn't mind a little thing like that.

His whiskers became white with the flour, and his black fur was flecked with the powdery stuff. He went on and on eating the flour, and only stopped when he heard Cook coming downstairs. Then he leapt out of the window, and as he went, he heard Cook shout out angrily.

"If that thief of a cat hasn't gone and snuffed up the self-raising flour!" she cried. "Well, it won't do him any good, I'm certain of that!"

Whiskers went and sat on a wall in the sun, and washed himself. It was while he was washing himself that he felt so funny. He stopped washing himself to think about the strange feeling that was coming over him. He felt as if he were suddenly very swollen and very light – rather like a balloon must feel when it is being blown up.

You see, the self-raising flour was beginning to act on him, just as it acts on cakes and bread. It makes them rise in the oven, and become nice and light to eat. Whiskers had sat himself down in the hot sun, and the flour was beginning to make him very light too.

"Whiskers and tails!" said the cat in alarm, digging his claws hard into the wall. "What's happening to me? I shall be floating up in the air in a minute, I feel so light and airy!"

And all at once he rose into the air! Up he went, clawing at the air, wondering whatever was going to happen. The sparrows who had been watching him from a nearby tree began to shout in surprise to each other.

"Chirrup, chirrup! Look at the cat! If he takes to flying in the air like us, we shan't have a chance to escape! Chirrup!"

They flew away in alarm and told the old jackdaw who lived in the church tower. He came at once to see the marvellous sight of a cat flying through the air, and when he saw poor old Whiskers, he cawed in delight.

"He's not flying!" he said. "He's gone up in the air like those round balloons do that the children play with. Oh my, what a game! Come on, boys, and we'll chase him!"

The sparrows were still too frightened to go near Whiskers, so the jackdaw fetched his friends the rooks, and all the

great black birds flew after Whiskers, who was still floating along in the air, getting higher and higher every minute.

He was very much afraid when he saw the birds coming after him, because he remembered how often he had chased some of them. He was just wondering what to do about it, when he floated over a smoking chimney, and the smoke got into his nose and eyes, and made him sneeze violently.

"Caw!" cried a rock, and pecked at his tail.

"Ka-kack!" said the jackdaw, and pulled out one of his hairs. Whiskers couldn't do anything, because as fast as he tried to claw at the birds, they dodged away, and pecked him somewhere else.

Whiskers rose higher and higher, and soon he was so high that the jackdaw and the rooks left him. He came to where the swallows and the martins were flying very high up, looking for insects. When they saw him they flew off in alarm, but one swallow saw that he was the cat who had frightened three of her babies the day before, and she flew at him and pecked off the end of one of his fine whiskers.

Then the others came up, and some swifts screeched so loudly in his ear that he jumped with fright, and found himself even higher than before.

Up he went, until he came to where an eagle soared round and round and round. Now Whiskers had never seen an eagle close to, and he had no idea what this enormous creature was. The eagle was astonished to see such a strange animal floating so high and swooped downwards to see him closely.

"This might be food for my eaglets," thought the great bird, circling round the frightened cat. He was just going to pounce when the self-raising flour stopped acting, and Whiskers found himself sinking quickly downwards. The eagle watched in astonishment, and decided not to catch him after all.

Down went Whiskers, and down, past the astonished swallows, and through a flock of alarmed starlings, who flew at him, and made him blink his eyes in fright.

Faster and faster, faster and faster! Then suddenly splash! He fell into the pond of water at the bottom of his own garden, and sent the ducks waddling helter-skelter away, quacking loudly. All except one duck – and she had a brood of little ones nearby, so she rushed angrily at Whiskers as he spluttered out of the water, and gave him such a punch with her beak that he fell back into the pond again.

Poor old Whiskers! He dragged himself off, and found a warm place in the sun to dry himself. It took him quite two hours to get dry, and all the sparrows flew down to a nearby tree, and made rude remarks to him.

And perhaps you won't be surprised to hear that Whiskers is a cat who *can* be trusted now. He never steals *anything*, and the cook can't think why! But *we* could tell her, couldn't we!

The big black cat

The big black cat from across the road used to sit on the wall and wait for Joan and Richard to come back from school.

He stood up and arched his back when he saw them coming. They ran up to him and stroked him, tickling his soft neck.

"You're a very nice cat," said Joan. "If you come into our garden this afternoon I'll give you a bit of fish. We're having fish for dinner, so there's sure to be a bit of skin for you off our plates."

The cat strolled into their garden almost every day. Sometimes the children gave him milk or little tit-bits. Sometimes they played with him, and

once he even went to sleep in Joan's doll's pram. That made Mummy laugh.

"Just look at that cat!" she said. "Anyone would think he belonged to you two children, not to Mrs Brown across the road."

The cat loved playing with the children's toys. He played ball very well. He liked running after Richard's clockwork train. He patted all the little dolls that sat in the train when they went for a ride.

Whenever he saw the children playing he went out to play with them. "Hallo, Blackie!" they would say, when he strolled into the garden. "Come along and play!"

But one day Richard played with something that Blackie couldn't catch or chase. He had a new aeroplane!

It was a lovely thing. It really could fly beautifully. It had to be wound up tightly with elastic, and then Richard held it high in the air, gave it a push off, and away it flew, whirring like a real aeroplane through the air. Sometimes it flew right down to the bottom of the garden.

The cat watched the aeroplane flying. It thought it must be some kind of toy bird. When it fell to the ground the cat went racing over to it, and pawed at it to make it fly again. But it wouldn't, of course, till Richard had wound up the elastic once more.

One day Richard flew the aeroplane when there was a very strong wind. It flew right up into the air and landed by the chimney. And there it stayed!

"Oh, dear," said Joan. "Look, Richard – it won't come back."

"It's stuck," said Richard, in dismay. "We must get a ladder."

But no ladder was long enough to reach up to the roof. Richard threw up a stick to try and dislodge the aeroplane, but Joan stopped him.

"No, don't do that – if the stick hits it, it will break a wing off the aeroplane

– and then it will never, never fly again."

"Well, what are we to do, then – leave it up there for ever and ever?" said Richard, sadly. He took a step backwards and trod on Blackie, who had been watching all this with great interest. Why didn't the aeroplane come back? Why did it like being up on the roof so much? Was there a bird's nest up there?

Blackie squealed when Richard trod on him. He bent down at once. "Oh, sorry, Blackie. Did I hurt you? I didn't see you there."

"Mee-ow," said Blackie, meaning that it didn't matter. He strolled up to a tree and sharpened his claws. Then up the tree he went in a bound, and on to the garage roof. He stopped to give himself a little wash, while he thought of what to do next.

Then he leapt up to the next roof, which led to the chimneys. Joan and Richard saw him.

"Look," said Joan. "Blackie's on the roof. I do hope he doesn't fall. I don't believe he's ever been on a roof before."

Blackie hadn't. He walked very carefully indeed. He climbed up the tiles to the chimney near to where the aeroplane rested. He came to it and sniffed at it.

"Blackie!" yelled Richard. "Blackie, be a clever cat – scrape at our aeroplane and get it down for us."

Blackie took no notice. He sniffed round, hoping to find a bird's nest. But there was none there, of course. He patted the aeroplane carefully. It moved just a little.

Blackie patted it again. He wanted it to fly as it usually did. Why wouldn't it? The wind came along and fluttered its tail. Blackie pounced on it. Up went the front part of the aeroplane as Blackie jumped at the tail, and the cat jumped back in alarm.

He nearly rolled down the tiles, but just managed to save himself. Joan squealed. Then Richard yelled loudly and made her jump.

"Look – Blackie has managed to get our aeroplane free – the wind's got it again – it's moving, it's moving!"

So it was! It slid down the roof a little way, and Blackie gave it a push. It slid all the way down the tiles with Blackie after it, came to the gutter, fell over it – and then glided down to earth through the air! It landed just by Richard.

"Oh, good cat, Blackie!" shouted Richard, in delight. "Clever cat! You've got my aeroplane back for me! Come down and we'll give you a treat!"

Blackie came down, pleased with himself. The children ran in and took some money from their money-box. Then they went to Mummy.

"Mummy," said Richard, "you've got some tins of sardines in your cupboard. Can we buy one for Blackie? He's just been very, very kind and good."

"Yes, if you like," said Mummy. "Whatever has he done?"

"He's climbed up on the roof, gone to the chimney, and set my aeroplane free for me," said Richard. "I really do think he deserves a treat."

Well, Blackie certainly enjoyed the sardines. He spent a whole hour afterwards washing himself. He wouldn't mind getting a dozen aeroplanes off the roof if he could have sardines as a reward!

And when the other cats smelt the sardine smell on him, and came round for a sniff, Blackie told them how he got such a treat – and, would you believe it, every time Joan and Richard fly that aeroplane now, at least half a dozen cats climb up to the roof and wait – just in *case* it gets stuck by the chimney again.

"I only hope it doesn't," says Richard, each time. "There wouldn't be much left of it if *all* those cats pounce on it to set it free!"

He needn't worry. Blackie will get there first!

The magic claws

There was once a gnome called Scruffy who found a magic spell by accident. It was a strange spell that had been lost for a great many years.

It was a spell to make pink claws for witch-cats! Witch-cats were never allowed to have claws, because they were quite powerful enough without wearing strong sharp claws too! So there had been for many years a law in Fairyland that no cat belonging to a witch should wear claws.

The spell to make claws had been buried deep in a wood – and Scruffy had found it by accident, when he was digging up a fern to sell.

He undid the string – and opened the

box he had found – and in it were two pink claws! Scruffy knew what they were at once – the claws that could work the spell to make others like themselves!

Now Scruffy should really have taken the box to the King – but he didn't. He knew he could make a lot of money for himself by selling witch-claws! So he took the box home, and began to practise the spell.

Very soon he had made twenty more pink claws, sharp and strong! Good! He packed them up and went to visit the witches at night. How pleased they were to buy the pink claws for their black cats! Now they would be able to catch rats again!

Scruffy sold all his claws that night. The next day he made twenty more – and sold those too. Goodness knows how many more he would have made and sold if something hadn't happened.

One of the witch-cats, fitted up nicely with strong pink claws, scratched a little pixie hurrying by to market. The pixie ran to the King and showed the long scratch down his little pink arm.

"The witch-cats have claws again, Your Majesty!" he cried. "Someone has found the old spell – and the witches are arming their cats with claws once more! What shall we do?"

"Call out the army!" ordered the King. "Call out the navy too – and the air force as well! I'll find the fairy who has the claw-spell before the day is out!"

So his army of rabbits marched up. His navy of frogs sailed up the stream. His air force of wasps and bees buzzed by in lines. Everything was ready!

Scruffy soon found out what was happening. He was frightened almost out of his life! He knew he would be severely punished if he was found with the claw-spell on him. What could he do?

"I'll run away!" he thought, in dismay. "Even if I throw away the spell, one of the witches will tell. I must go!"

So he packed up his bag and left at once. He ran out of the gates of Fairyland and didn't stop until he sat down under a hedge in our world. He was hot and tired. He was sad and homesick.

Above him were some pink wild roses. They scented the air and made everything sweet. The bush spoke to him.

"Why do you weep, little gnome?"

The gnome told his story, and showed the pink claws that belonged to the spell. The bush waved about in excitement.

"Little gnome, those claws are just what I want! My stems are not strong enough to stand up by themselves, so they have to lean on other bushes, and very often I cannot get high enough to feel the sunshine on me. If only you would give me some of those pink claws to set all the way up my stems, I could use them to climb with – and I would soon be at the top of the bushes, waving about in the sunshine!"

Scruffy was surprised to hear this. He looked closely at the bush. It was quite true, the stems were very weak and could not stand upright by themselves as those of other bushes did.

Scruffy was glad to please anyone, he felt so sad and ashamed. He set to work to make the spell once more.

Under his hands appeared the magic pink claws – one, two, three, four – twelve, fifteen, twenty! There they lay in a little heap, ready to be used. But not for witch-cats this time! No – Scruffy was not going to sell them, he was going to give them away.

He took up the sharp, curved claws. He went to a stem and, pressing a claw into it, he muttered a magic word that made it grow. Hey presto, the claw stayed there! Then Scruffy took up the next pink claw and did the same thing. It grew on the stem in a trice.

All the twenty claws were soon used – and Scruffy had to make some more for the grateful wild rose bush. It was not long before all the stems were neatly set with strong magic claws. The bush was glad. She used them as hooks to help herself climb higher up. Now she would always be able to reach the golden sunshine.

"Thank you, little gnome," she said gratefully. "You are very clever. You have done me a good turn today. Stay here in our world and help my brothers and sisters too!"

Scruffy never went back to Fairyland. He is still here with us, fitting the wild rose stems with pink claws. Have you seen them? Do look! You will find them growing all the way up the stem, strong, curved cats' claws! Pick a few off carefully and make a wish. There may be enough magic in them to make a wish come true. You never know!

Nobby's school

Nobby the gnome has a dear little
  school
For kittens and froggies and rabbits.
He stands by his blackboard out there
  in the wood
And teaches them all kinds of habits.

The froggies learn just how to flick out
  their tongues
To catch any flies that appear,
The rabbits are taught to show bobtails
  of white
As a signal that danger is near!

The kittens learn purring, and mewing
  as well,
And how to put claws out and in –
Really the school is an excellent one,
With *plenty* of prizes to win!

A tale of the blue-eyed cat

"**I** wish," said the black cat loudly, "I do wish that the pink rabbit would go to some other toy cupboard to live."

The black cat was a toy cat. She wasn't much bigger than a small kitten, but she was as grown-up as a cat in her ways.

The pink rabbit glared at the toy cat. "And *I* wish," he said, "that silly black cat with blue eyes would go and jump out of the window. *Blue* eyes! Whoever heard of blue eyes for a cat? Cats have green ones."

"Now, now," said the teddy bear. "Don't start squabbling again, you two. You really ought to behave better, Rabbit, because you are much older

than the toy cat."

The pink rabbit scowled. He was dressed very smartly in blue velvet trousers and a red coat. On his coat were three glass buttons, as green as grass. The pink rabbit was very proud of them.

"Look!" he said to the cat, pointing to his gleaming glass buttons. "Why haven't you got eyes as green as my buttons? Fancy having *blue* eyes!"

"Be quiet, Rabbit. She can't help it," said the big doll. "I've got blue eyes, too."

"It's nice in a doll," said the rabbit. "And look at that cat's tail, too – all the hairs have come off at the end!"

"Well, she couldn't help the puppy chewing her tail," said the bear. "Don't be so mean and bad-tempered, Rabbit."

That was the worst of Rabbit. He *was* so mean. If anyone did anything he didn't like, he said mean things and played nasty tricks, too, on anybody who annoyed him. When the bear grumbled at him one day, he hid behind the curtain with a big pin. And as soon as the bear came along, Rabbit pinned him to the curtain so that he couldn't get away. That was the sort of thing he did.

So nobody liked him much, and they all thought him vain and silly.

The black cat disliked him very much. If she could she always turned her back on him, and he didn't like that.

"Stuck-up creature!" he grumbled. "With her silly blue ribbon and great, staring blue eyes."

One day the toy cat found a piece of chocolate dropped on the floor. She was very pleased. She bit it into many small pieces, and gave a bit to all her friends. But she didn't give even a lick to the rabbit.

"Mean thing!" he said, when he saw everyone munching chocolate. "All right; you just wait. I'll pay you back some day, yes, I will!"

Now, the next week, the black cat felt worried. She couldn't see properly out of one of her blue eyes. She told the bear about it and he had a look at the eye.

"Goodness! It's coming loose!" he said. "I hope Mary notices it, Cat, or it may drop off and be lost. You'd look funny with only one eye."

Mary was the little girl in whose

playroom they all lived. The toy cat kept staring at her, hoping she would notice her loose eye. But she didn't.

Mary had just got a new book and she couldn't stop reading it. You know how it is when you have an exciting book. You just want to go on and on reading.

So the toy cat's eye got looser and looser. At last it was hanging by only one thread, and still Mary hadn't noticed it. She was nearly at the end of her book, though, and the cat hoped maybe her eye would hold on till Mary had finished reading. Then she would be sure to notice her toy cat's eye.

But that night, after Mary had gone to bed, the cat's eye dropped right off! She had been sitting quite still, afraid she might jerk it off – and then she had forgotten to keep still and had run across the room to speak to the bear.

She felt her eye falling out. It fell on the floor with a little thud – and then it rolled away under the couch! The cat gave a cry.

"Oh, my eye's gone! It's under the couch. Please get it, somebody!"

The toys all lay down and peeped under the couch. All except the rabbit. *He* wasn't going to bother himself! But suddenly he saw, quite near his foot, something that shone blue. He stared at it. Gracious, it was the toy cat's eye! It must have rolled under the couch and out at the other side, and have come right over to where the rabbit sat looking at a picture book!

He looked at the other toys. They were all lying on the floor, poking about under the couch. The toy cat was watching, crying tears out of her one eye.

Quick as lightning the rabbit put his foot over the blue glass eye. He kicked it into a corner. Then he got up, went to the corner and, without anybody noticing, put the eye into his pocket.

"Now I've got the cat's eye!" he thought. "Good! She won't get it back again, that's certain. I'll pay her back now for all the things she said to me!"

He went over to the toys and pretended to look for the eye with them. But all the time he could feel it in his pocket. He wanted to laugh.

"Perhaps I'd better hide it safely somewhere," he thought suddenly. "If any of the toys found out that I had the eye, I should get into dreadful trouble. They might turn me out of the playroom. Now, where can I put it?"

Well, you will never guess where he hid it! It really was a very clever place. He went into the dolls' house. There was nobody there, for all the dolls were helping the cat to look for her dropped eye.

He went into the kitchen. He lifted up the lid of the tiny kettle set on the toy stove – and he dropped the eye in there. It just went in nicely.

Then he put the lid on and ran out quietly. Nobody would ever, ever find the eye now, because the dolls' house dolls never used that kettle. They had a smaller one they liked better.

The toy cat was very miserable indeed. She cried bitterly. The toys tried to comfort her. Only the pink rabbit didn't say anything nice. He was glad.

"How mean and unkind you are, Rabbit," said everyone.

But he didn't care a bit.

The next day Mary finished her book, and had time to look at her toys again. And, of course, she noticed at once that the toy cat had only one eye. She was very upset.

"You look *dreadful!*" she said. "You must have dropped it. I'll look around for it." But she couldn't find it, of course, because it was in the kettle.

"Whatever shall I do with you?" said Mary to the miserable toy cat. "You can't go about with one eye, that's certain. And I haven't a blue button that would do for you. What *can* I do?"

She looked at all the other toys, and she suddenly saw the pink rabbit, dressed so smartly in his velvet coat and trousers, with the three gleaming green buttons on his coat.

"Oh! Of *course*. *I* know what to do," cried Mary; and she picked up the surprised rabbit. "You can have *two* new eyes, Toy Cat – proper green ones, this time! I'll take off your old blue one, and put on two of these beautiful green ones. You will look simply lovely!"

Well, what do you think of that? *Snip, snip*, went Mary's scissors, and, to the pink rabbit's horror, the two top buttons of his coat fell off.

Then Mary took off the one blue eye of the toy cat, and put on the two green ones instead. You can't imagine how handsome the cat looked, with two gleaming green eyes, instead of blue ones. She stared round at the toys in delight.

The toy cat looked lovely but the pink rabbit felt cross and unhappy. He had lost his beautiful green buttons and that awful toy cat had got them instead. She was looking at him with his own buttons for eyes. The rabbit could hardly stop himself from crying with rage.

Now, the toys might have been sorry for the rabbit, and tried to comfort him, if something else hadn't happened just then. Mary suddenly decided to give a party for the toy cat to celebrate her beautiful new eyes. And she took the kettle off the toy stove to fill with water so that she might boil it for tea.

And inside she found the blue eye of the toy cat. She picked it out in the very greatest astonishment. She looked at it, and so did all the toys.

"*Who* put that here?" said Mary

Nobody said anything. But something strange happened to the rabbit's pink face. It turned a dark red. Everyone stared at him in surprise, and then they knew who had hidden the blue eye. It was the naughty pink rabbit.

"So *you* hid it," said Mary. "You naughty, mean toy. I suppose you think I'm going to take off the toy

cat's green eyes and give them back to you as buttons now that we have two blue eyes for her again. But I'm not. She can keep her green eyes now. She looks very beautiful with them. As for you, it was a *very good punishment* to lose your lovely buttons. And, what is more, you shan't come to the party."

"Oh, let him come," said the toy cat, so happy now because she had such beautiful green eyes that she simply couldn't be unkind to anyone. "Let him come. I'll forgive him. Give him a chance to be nice."

So he came. But he was very quiet, and sad and well-behaved.

The toys all think he may be better now. But he does feel strange when he sees the toy cat staring at him through the buttons he once wore on his own coat.

Whiskers for the cat

In the corner of the playroom there was a small rocking horse. He was only half the usual size, but the smaller children liked him because he just fitted them nicely.

He had big rockers and he creaked a little when the children rode him. "*Cree-eek, cree-eek*," he said. And the toys got quite used to the noise.

"I'm the only toy in this playroom big enough for the children to ride on," boasted the little rocking horse. "I ought to be King of the playroom."

"Well, you won't be," said the curly-haired doll. "You squashed the monkey's tail yesterday, and that was unkind."

"I didn't mean to," said the horse, offended. "He shouldn't have left it lying about under my rockers. Silly of him."

"You should have looked down before you began to rock, and you would have seen it," said the doll.

"Well, do you suppose I'm going to bother to look for tails and things before I begin to rock?" said the horse. "You just look out for yourselves! That's the best thing to do."

But the toys were careless. Once the little red toy motor car ran under the horse's rockers, and was squashed

almost flat. And another time the clockwork clown left his key there and the rocking horse bent it when he rocked on it. It was difficult to wind up the clown after that, and he was cross.

Then the baby doll dropped her bead necklace and the rocking horse rocked on it and smashed the beads. The toys were really very angry with him about that.

"Why did you rock just then? Only because you knew you would break the beads!" they cried. "You are really very unkind. We shan't speak to you or play with you."

"Don't then," said the horse, and he rocked away by himself. *"Cree-eek, creek-eek!* I'm sure I don't want to talk to you *or* give you rides if you are so cross and silly."

After that nobody took any notice of the little rocking horse. The worst of it was that Johnny, the little boy who often rode him, went away to stay with his granny for a long time, so nobody rode the horse at all. It was very dull for him.

"I wish they'd talk to me!" thought the horse sadly. "I wish they'd play. I'd like to give them each a ride – in fact, I'd take three of them at once if they asked me."

But the toys acted as if the rocking horse wasn't there at all. They didn't ask him anything. They didn't even look at him.

"He's unkind and selfish and horrid," they said. "And the best way to treat people like that is not to take any notice of them."

So the rocking horse got duller and duller, and he longed to gallop round the playroom just for a change. But he was afraid the toys might be cross if he did.

Now one day the puppy came into the playroom, because someone had left the door open. The toys fled to the toy cupboard in fear, because the puppy was very playful and liked to carry a toy outside and chew it.

Everyone got safely into the cupboard except the black cat. She slipped and fell, and the puppy pounced on her. He chewed her black head and nibbled her whiskers away. Nobody dared to rescue her, not even the rocking horse, though he did wonder if he should gallop at the puppy.

Then somebody whistled and the puppy flew out of the door and downstairs. The poor black cat sat up. "My head does feel chewed!" she said. "And oh – what's happened to my fine black whiskers?"

"They've gone," said the teddy bear, peeping out of the cupboard. "The puppy has chewed them off. There they are, look, on the floor, in tiny little bits."

The black cat cried bitterly. She had been proud of her whiskers. "A cat doesn't look like a cat without her whiskers," she wept. "What shall I do? Can I get any more?"

Well, the toys did try their very hardest to get her some whiskers, but there were none to be found anywhere. And then a humble voice came from the corner where the little rocking horse stood.

"Excuse me, toys – but I've got an idea."

"It's only the rocking horse," said the teddy bear. "Don't take any notice of him."

"Please do take some notice," said the horse. "I've got a *good* idea. I should be very pleased to give the toy cat some of the hairs out of my long white tail. They would do beautifully for whiskers."

There was a silence after this. Then the toy cat stood up. "Well! That's a very good idea indeed, and *very* kind of you!" she said, and she walked over to the horse. "But how can I get some hairs from your tail?"

"Pull them out, of course," said the horse.

"But it will hurt you," said the toy cat.

"I don't mind," said the horse, bravely, "pull as many as you like!" So the toy cat pulled seven out, and they did hurt. But the horse didn't make a sound.

Then the curly-haired doll threaded a big needle with one of the hairs and ran it gently through the toy cat's cheeks. "One whisker!" she said. She threaded the needle again. "Two whiskers! Three whiskers! Oh, you will look fine, Toy Cat. These are white whiskers, long and strong, and you will look very, very beautiful now."

"I must say it was nice of the rocking horse to give you them," said the teddy bear, suddenly. "Especially as we haven't even spoken to him lately. Very nice of him."

Everyone thought the same. So when the toy cat's new whiskers were all in place, and she looked very fine indeed, the toys went with her to show her to the rocking horse.

"Very good idea of yours!" said the curly-haired doll.

"Very kind of you," said the teddy bear.

"I can't thank you enough!" said the black cat. "I had black whiskers before, and they didn't show up very well – but these show beautifully. Don't you think so?"

"You look lovely," said the horse. "Very lovely."

"Your tail looks a bit thin now, I'm afraid," said the toy cat. "Do you mind?"

"Not a bit," said the rocking horse. "I can rock to and fro just as fast when my tail is thin as when it's thick. You get on my back and see, Black Cat!"

So up got the black cat, and the rocking horse went rocking round the playroom at top speed. It was very exciting. You may be sure the horse looked where he was going! He wasn't going to rock over anyone's tail again!

"Oh, thank you!" said the toy cat, quite out of breath. "That was the nicest ride I ever had!"

"Anyone can have one!" said the

horse, rather gruffly, because he was afraid that the toys might say 'No', and turn their backs on him.

But they didn't. They all climbed up at once. "Nice old horse!" they said. "We're friends again now, aren't we? Gallop away, gallop away!"

And you should have seen him gallop away again.

The lost doll's pram

"Mummy, I do so wish Tibbles wouldn't keep jumping into my doll's pram," said Eileen. "How can I stop her?"

"Well, you could stop her by doing what *I* used to do, when you were a baby in your pram," said Mummy. "You can put a net over the pram so that no cat can jump into it."

"Oh dear – I don't want to do that," said Eileen. "It would be an awful bother to have to do that every time I put my dolls to sleep. I shall shout at Tibbles next time I find her in my doll's pram!"

Eileen found her there the very next morning, curled up under the

eiderdown, fast asleep. Shout! Tibbles gave a meow of surprise, and leapt out at once. She was never shouted at by Eileen and she didn't like it at all.

"You are *not* to get into the pram," said Eileen to Tibbles. "I have told you ever so often. You are a naughty little cat. Do you want to smother Rosebud or Josephine, by lying on top of them? Shoo! Go away!"

Tibbles ran away – but will you believe it, as soon as Eileen went indoors again, Tibbles jumped right into the pram once more!

She did love that pram. It was so soft inside and so cosy. She loved cuddling down, curling herself up and going to sleep in peace and quiet there.

"It just fits me nicely," she thought. "I can share it with the dolls. They never seem to mind. They don't even kick me."

Now the next day three naughty boys came along with a naughty little girl. They saw some apples hanging on the trees in Eileen's garden, and they crept in at the gate to take some.

Eileen saw them from the window. She rushed out into the garden. "You bad children! That's stealing! Go away and leave my daddy's apples alone."

"Give us some!" shouted the biggest boy.

"No, certainly not. If you had come to ask my daddy properly, he would have given you a basketful," cried Eileen. "But people who steal don't get any. Go away!"

"You're a horrid little girl!" shouted the boy. "We'll pay you back!"

And then Eileen's mother came out and the four naughty children ran away. They came peeping over the wall again the day after – but not to take the apples. They meant to pay Eileen back for sending them away.

"Look – there's her doll's pram," whispered the little girl. "Let's take it away into the park and hide it where she can't find it. That will teach her to shout at us and send us away. Quick, Bill – there's no one about – you slip in and get it."

Bill opened the back gate, ran into the garden and took hold of the pram handles. He wheeled the little pram at top speed out of the gate. Slam! – the gate shut, and the four children hurried down the lane to the park.

"She hasn't got any dolls in the pram," said the little girl. "I'd have thrown them into the bushes if she had!"

What a very horrid little girl she was! She had dolls of her own and loved them – and yet she would have done an unkind thing to someone else's dolls! Well, well – some people are strange, aren't they?

The boys stuffed the pram into the middle of a big bush and left it there. Then they went back to Eileen's garden to see what she said when she came out and found her pram missing.

She soon came out with her two dolls, meaning to take them for a walk, as she always did each morning. But where was her pram? It was nowhere to be seen! Eileen looked everywhere for it – and then she saw the four heads of the giggling children, peeping over the wall.

"Have you seen my pram?" she called.

"Yes," they called back.

"Where is it?" shouted Eileen.

"It's hidden in the park where you can't find it!" called the biggest boy. "Ha, ha! You'll never find it again!"

"Mummy, Mummy, come here!" called Eileen, almost in tears. But her mother had just gone next door and she didn't come. So Eileen had to make up her mind herself what she was going to do.

"I must go and look in the park," she thought. "Oh, dear – suppose it rains? My lovely pram will be soaked. Suppose I don't find it? How am I to know where those bad children have put it?"

She put her dolls down just inside the house, ran down the garden again, into the lane and was soon in the park. Now – where should she look?

She hunted here and she hunted there. She looked in this bush and that, but she couldn't find her pram.

"Oh, dear – there are such a lot of bushes and trees!" thought poor Eileen. "I could look all day long and never find my pram. Where *can* it be?"

It was very well hidden indeed. Someone else was well-hidden there too. And that was Tibbles!

Tibbles had been in the pram when the bad children had run off with it, curled up as usual under the eiderdown, fast asleep. When the children had taken the pram, Tibbles had thought it was Eileen taking the dolls for a walk. She hadn't dared to pop her head up, in case Eileen was cross with her. So she just lay there, wondering why the pram went so fast that morning. Then suddenly it was pushed into the bushes, and was still. Tibbles shut her eyes and went to sleep again.

She woke up after a time and stretched herself. Everything seemed very quiet. Tibbles felt hungry and thought she would jump out of the pram and go and find her dinner. She had forgotten that the pram had been taken for a walk – she thought she was still in garden!

She poked her head out from under the covers and looked round. What was this? She was somewhere quite strange! This wasn't her garden. Tibbles sat right up, very frightened.

Where was she? Where was Eileen? What had happened? And dear me, was this rain beginning to fall?

It was. Big drops pattered down on Tibbles, and she crouched down. She hated the rain. She suddenly felt very lonely and frightened and she gave a loud meow.

"MEOW! MEE-OW-EE-OW-EE-OW-EE-OW!"

Nothing happened except that the rain pattered down more loudly. One enormous drop fell splash on to Tibbles' nose, and she meowed angrily.

The rain made a loud noise on the bracken around, and Tibbles couldn't think what it was. She didn't dare to jump out of the pram.

"MEEOW-OW-OW!" she wailed, at the top of her voice.

Eileen was not very far off, and she heard this last MEE-OW. She stopped. That sounded like a cat's voice! Was there a cat lost in the park, caught in the rain that was now pouring down? Poor thing!

"MEEEEEEEEE-OOOW-OOOOW!" wailed Tibbles, and Eileen hurried towards the sound. "MEEE-OW!"

"It seems to come from that bush over there," thought the little girl, and went to it. Another loud wail came from the spot.

"Meee-ow-ow-ow! MEE-ow-ow-OW!"

And then Eileen suddenly saw the handles of her pram sticking out of the bush. How delighted she was! She ran to them and gave a tug – out came her doll's pram – and there, sitting in the middle of it, scared and lonely, was Tibbles!

"Oh, *Tibbles*! It was you I heard meowing!" cried Eileen, in surprise. "You must have been asleep in the pram again when those children ran off with it. Oh, Tibbles, I *am* glad you were in it – it was your meowing that made me find it! I'll never scold you again for getting into the pram!"

She put up the hood, and drew the waterproof cover over Tibbles so that the frightened cat shouldn't get soaked. And then off she went home with her precious pram, not minding the rain in the least because she was so pleased to have found her pram again.

Tibbles couldn't imagine why Eileen made such a fuss of her, but she liked it all the same. The funny thing was that she never, never got into the doll's pram again. She was so afraid it would run off with her into the park and lose her!

So do you know what she does? She gets into the doll's cot up in the playroom and goes to sleep there! I've seen her, and she really does look sweet, curled up with her tail round her nose.

Smokey and the seagull

"I wish my mistress wouldn't put my dinner out of doors," said Smokey the cat to his friend Sooty. Smokey was on the wall with him, and their long tails hung down, twitching just a little.

"Why? What does it matter if she does?" said Sooty. "It tastes just the same, indoors or out!"

"I know. But there's a big seagull that comes in from the beach," said Smokey, "and he sits on our roof and watches for my mistress to come out with my dinner – it's always a nice bit of fish, you know – and that seagull loves fish! And as soon as he sees my mistress coming out with my dish, down he flies to it – and gobbles up my dinner!"

"Well! I wonder you allow that!" said Sooty, swinging his black tail angrily, as he thought of the greedy seagull. "I have *my* dinner indoors, thank goodness!"

"My mistress won't let me have it there," said Smokey, sadly. "She says

I make too much mess. So what am I to do?"

"Pounce on the seagull, of course," said Sooty. "That's easy."

"Sooty – have you ever *seen* a seagull close to?" asked Smokey. "Do you know how *big* it is?"

"No. I never go down on the beach," said Sooty. "I don't like walking in soft sand – it's like snow, and my paws sink right down."

"Well – a seagull is *enormous*," said Smokey. "I wouldn't *dare* to pounce on it."

"Well, just pounce on its tail, then," said Sooty. "And hang on for all your worth. Pull out a few feathers if you can – then that seagull won't come again!"

"Yes – that may be quite a good idea," said Smokey. "It is its beak I'm scared of – it's so big and strong. I really believe it could bite off my tail!"

"Well, you get hold of the seagull's tail first!" said Sooty. "I'll sit up here and cheer you on. Do be brave, Smokey."

"That's all very well," said Smokey. "*You'd* think twice before you pounced on a great seagull! Still – I'll try it. I'll hide behind the dustbin and wait till the gull comes down. Then, when it has its back to me – I'll pounce!"

"What time do you have your dinner?" asked Sooty. "I really must watch this."

"When that big clock over there strikes *one*," said Smokey. "Mistress comes out just after that. Sooty, will you come to my help if I need it?"

"Of course. Certainly!" said Sooty. "I'll leap right on top of it."

"You *are* brave!" said Smokey, admiringly. "All right – watch out for my mistress to come at dinner time."

He jumped down from the wall, and ran off to the house. Just before he went indoors he looked up at the sky. There were the big seagulls, gliding to and fro on the breeze, their enormous wings spread wide. Smokey wondered which of them was the one that stole his dinner!

He smelt his fish cooking on the kitchen stove, and felt hungry. Yesterday the seagull had gobbled all his dinner up, and poor Smokey had only been able to lick out the dish. How he hoped he would be able to eat it all himself today!

"Are you hungry, little cat?" asked his mistress. "Well, you shall have your fish as soon as it is cool. Don't keep walking round and round my legs like that – it won't make your dinner come any quicker!"

When the big clock struck one, Sooty jumped up on to the wall to see if Smokey really *did* mean to pounce on the seagull. He saw his friend come running out of the house and then he hid behind the dustbin. Only the tip of his whiskers could be seen.

Overhead a big gull spread its white wings and waited for Smokey's dinner to arrive!

Sooty gazed up at it and felt quite scared when he saw how big it was.

Goodness – would Smokey be brave enough to pounce on that enormous bird?

Smokey saw the gull too and hissed and spat. That greedy gull! Well, Smokey meant to pounce on him if he possibly could. He saw Sooty up on the wall, watching. He would show him how brave he was!

Smokey's mistress came out with his dish of fish. How good it smelt!

"Smokey, Smokey!" she called. "Dinner! Where are you?"

Smokey stayed behind the dustbin, waiting. His mistress went indoors.

As soon as she had disappeared the big seagull glided down on outspread wings. It landed on the lawn, and closed its wings, then walked quickly over to the dish, turning its back on Smokey. It was just about to peck up a large mouthful of fish when Smokey shot out from his hiding-place, and pounced on the seagull's tail.

The gull was very frightened. It gave

a loud cry, spread its wings and rose
up into the air – and what a sight
to see – it took poor Smokey with
it!

You see, Smokey hadn't had time to
let go of the tail, and there he was, up in

the air with the gull, hanging on to the tail-feathers for dear life!

Sooty watched in amazement. *Now* what would happen? Poor Smokey! Would he be taken right out to sea, and shaken off into the big waves?

The seagull was just as frightened as Smokey. It took a quick look round and saw that the heavy weight on its tail was a little black cat! It didn't know what to do! It couldn't peck him off in mid-air.

And then something most peculiar happened. The tail-feathers could no longer bear the weight of the cat – and they broke off! So, of course, poor Smokey fell from the seagull, the tail-feathers still in his mouth and claws, and found himself falling, falling, through the air. He was very frightened – and Sooty, on the wall, meowed in horror.

But, like all cats, Smokey landed on his feet. He found himself on the lawn, very shaken and surprised, but unhurt.

He sat down to get his breath, his mouth full of white tail-feathers! Sooty called out to him.

"Smokey! Are you hurt? My – aren't you brave!"

Smokey spat out the tail-feathers, and looked proudly at Sooty. "Well – I won, didn't I? I've saved my dinner – and pulled out the seagull's tail-feathers, though I didn't really mean to. I *was* surprised when he flew up into the air with me."

"Good old Smokey!" said Sooty. "I really *must* tell all the other cats about this. Come with me, Smokey. You'll be a hero!"

"No. I want my dinner before I'm a hero," said Smokey and ran to his dish. He gobbled up all the fish, and didn't even bother to keep a look-out for the seagull – no – he had beaten him for always! That gull would never dare to come back.

Smokey was right. The big seagull kept well away from gardens after that. Sooty and Smokey sat on the wall, looking up into the sky day after day – and how they meowed when they saw a gull without a tail!

"There he is! *Meow-meow!* How strange he looks. We'll always know him now."

But they won't. The seagull's tail feathers are already growing again, and soon he will look just like the others. What a shock he had that day when Smokey pounced on his tail – and what a hero Smokey is now!

The careless kitten

There was once a madcap of a kitten. It just simply didn't care what it did! It leapt here and it leapt there, it ran up the curtains, it hid under the bed, it got between people's feet and tripped them over.

The kitten's mother lived next door and was always hearing tales of the madcap kitten of hers.

"Do you know, the kitten jumped into the pond today," cried the big dog. "Splash it went! It was after the goldfish, silly little thing."

"And will you believe it, it scratched the big dog up the road," chirped a sparrow. "*Scratched* it! Well, if the kitten hadn't leapt up a tree at once it would have been bitten! It won't last long at that rate."

The kitten's mother was very worried. She spoke to the dog. "That's twice the kitten has almost lost its life," she said. "Twice! It's only got seven lives now, and it's hardly four months old."

"Seven lives left – what do you mean?" asked the dog.

"Well, didn't you know that all cats have nine lives?" said the cat. "I suppose you poor dogs have only one. Well, we have nine – and I'm so afraid my kitten is using hers up too quickly. Once nearly drowned – once nearly bitten by

117

a dog – that's two lives gone in a week."

"I'll warn her," said the dog.

But before he could say anything the kitten climbed up to the roof of the house and fell right off it to the ground! The dog ran up to see if she was hurt – but no, she leapt up and ran off, laughing at the dog.

"That's three lives gone!" called the dog. "Come here, I want to talk to you."

But the kitten was cheeky and ran away.

The dog watched for her, and he saw her in the road the very next day. He ran to tell her what her mother had said – but before he could reach her the little thing ran straight out into the road. A car came along and the kitten disappeared under it.

"Well, it will be killed for certain," thought the dog.

But no, it came out from under the car as frisky as ever. Not one of the wheels had touched it.

"Hey, that's four lives gone!" barked

the dog. "Will you please come here, you silly little thing. I've a message from your mother."

"I don't want to hear it," mewed the kitten. "Mummy's always telling me off. Go away."

She ran up a tree and the dog couldn't get near her. He barked at the bottom. The kitten ran down, patted him on the nose and ran off in front of him.

He ran after her, determined to make her listen. But she ran straight up a tall flag-pole, to the very, very top!

And, of course, she couldn't get down! When she tried to get down she lost her balance and fell – right on top of the surprised dog!

He tried to grab her in his mouth, but she was off again at once.

"Listen! That's *five* lives gone!" barked the dog anxiously. "Do, do listen to me."

But the kitten wouldn't. She ran into the house and the dog couldn't follow.

A week later he saw the kitten again.

She was prancing about round a horse's hooves. Down came a hoof just missing the little thing's head.

"Another life gone," groaned the dog. "Only three more left. She'll have lost them all before I can warn her."

Then the kitten lost two more lives very quickly indeed. She jumped up on a pile of books and they all toppled over on her, almost squashing her. Then, in a great fright, she rushed up to the bathroom to where Sammy, the little boy, was having a bath, and jumped straight into the water to be with him!

Sammy's mummy brought down the kitten to dry her in the sun. She was wet through and frightened. Mummy put her down by the big dog.

"Look after the poor little thing for me," she said. "She's nearly killed herself by overbalancing a great pile of books and then by leaping into Sammy's bath water. Get a little sense into her head, Rover."

"Eight lives lost," said the big dog,

and he licked the kitten gently. She was very, very wet.

"What's all this you keep saying about lives being lost?" she asked.

So Rover told her. "You've got nine lives, like any cat – and you're throwing them all away, one by one. You've lost eight of your lives already. You've only got one left to last you now. What are you going to do about it?"

"Good gracious, why didn't somebody tell me this before?" cried the kitten in alarm. "I shall be very, very careful now. I shall lose my silly ways and grow into a sensible, well-behaved cat."

So she did – and everyone said, "Oh, what a pity that kittens so soon grow up and lose their playful ways and turn into solemn cats."

Well, now you'll know why they do – it's because somebody suddenly tells them about their nine lives, and they decide not to waste any more! How many lives has *your* cat lost? Mine's lost about five already.

Midnight tea party

I peeped one night in the
   playroom,
And I was surprised to see
The pussycat and the teddy
Having their friends to tea!

The clockwork mouse and old Jumbo,
The sailor doll and the clown,
And all the dolls from the dolls' house
At the table were sitting down.

Pussy had borrowed my tea set,
And Teddy was cutting a cake,
There were jellies a-shake in the dishes,
And crackers for each one to take.

You think I was dreaming? I wasn't!
Today I found crumbs on the mat,
And jelly in one of the dishes,
And the pussycat's blue paper hat!

123

Duffy does his best

Duffy and his sister Dumpy lived together in a dear little house with Paddy the cat. Dumpy was called Dumpy because she was short and plump – but nobody knew why Duffy was called Duffy.

Dumpy kept house for Duffy, and she did it very well. Duffy wasn't really much help. He always got in the way, and he so often forgot the jobs he was meant to do.

"I really don't know what would happen to you, Duffy, if I went away for a holiday," said Dumpy, one day. "You'd forget to do the shopping, you'd never make your bed, and as for the cat I think she'd run away, because

I know you'd never think she was hungry!"

"Really, my dear, you shouldn't say such silly things," said Duffy, quite cross. "I'm quite capable of looking after myself and the house, and Paddy, and I could do it just as well as you do. So there!"

"Well, I'd like to go out this afternoon," said Dumpy. "But there are a few things that must be done, and I'm not sure I can trust you to do them. So I think I won't go out."

"How ridiculous you are!" said Duffy, very much annoyed. "As if I can't remember to do a few things for you! Just tell me what they are and I'll write them down, so that I shall easily remember. And when you come back, my dear, you will find them all done just as well as *you* could do them!"

"All right, Duffy," said Dumpy. "Now listen – there are four things. The first is, I've made a cake. It is over there, cooling. Please put it on a dish and put it on the tea table at half-past four, because I shall bring old Mrs Do-a-Lot home with me and I'd like her to see a nice tea all ready for her. I've laid the table – it just needs the cake on a dish."

"Easy," said Duffy, scribbling down a note in his notebook. "Remember cake."

"The next thing is, please give the cat her dinner when she comes in," said Dumpy. "She's gone off somewhere and she'll be very hungry. Take the fish out of the larder and put it on her dish for her when she comes in."

"Fish on dish," Duffy said and wrote it down carefully. "What next? These things are easy!"

"Well, a boy will come to fetch the kitchen clock," said Dumpy. "It wants mending. Look, I'll stand it here down by the kitchen door, ready for you to give to him. Just hand it out and say it's for Mr Tick-Tock."

"Right," said Duffy, and wrote down 'clock to go away'.

"And the last thing is, could you just put the tea leaves in the dustbin for me when you go into the garden?" said Dumpy. "It's raining at the moment and I don't want to get my feet wet."

"Right," said Duffy again, and wrote quickly in his notebook. " 'Tea leaves'. That will remind me to put them into the dustbin for you. There, my dear, now you can get ready to go out, knowing that all these jobs will be done for you without fail. You needn't worry at all! I can't forget because I've got them all written down!"

"Thank you, Duffy," said Dumpy, and off she went to get ready. Soon she said goodbye and trotted out happily. Duffy waved to her, feeling very good and helpful.

He thought he would like to listen to the radio for a little while. There was a cricket match on somewhere and he liked listening to cricket. His sister Dumpy didn't like it, so he didn't often listen to it. Now he would really enjoy himself!

He turned on the radio, and settled himself down in a chair to listen. He patted the notebook in his pocket. "I've got everything written down. I can't possibly forget," he thought. "As soon as I switch off the radio I will set to work to do everything Dumpy told me."

He listened for a whole hour. Then the cricket was ended so he turned the radio off, got up and stretched himself.

"Very fine cricket," he said. "Now, let me see . . . what did I have to do? I've quite forgotten! Oh dear. Something about that cake over there, I know. Now what did Dumpy tell me about it? Had she made it for somebody? I'll just look and see if there's any cake in the cake tin. If there is she must have made the fresh one for somebody. But who would it be?"

He looked in the cake tin. There was a sponge sandwich there. He scratched his head. "Well now, Dumpy must have meant me to give that cake to someone. What *was* I to do with it?"

He took out his notebook and looked at it. "I've written 'remember cake'," he said. "Well, I've remembered it, but that's about all. Hello – there's somebody at the door."

He went to the door. A small boy was there. He grinned up at Duffy. "I've been sent to collect something," he said.

"Ah! Was it a cake?" asked Duffy at once.

"I wasn't told," said the boy. "But I've brought a basket with me."

"Then it must be the cake," said Duffy, happily. "I'll get it. Half a minute." He took the nicely cooled cake and put it into a paper bag. The boy took it, delighted, and popped it in the basket. "My dad *will* be pleased," he said. "Thank you very much, sir."

"I hope you enjoy it," said Duffy, and shut the door. "Well, that's one thing remembered," he thought to himself.

"Now, what's next on my list of things to do."

He looked at his notebook. " 'Fish on dish'. Ha, fish on dish! Now what does that mean? What dish am I to put it on?"

He saw the empty cake dish on the tea table. Was that the dish for the fish? There didn't seem to be any other dish set ready to be filled. Dumpy must have told him to put the fish on that dish. He went to the larder and looked inside. There was a large cooked herring on an enamel plate. There was no other fish to be seen.

"Well, Herring, you must go on the dish," said Duffy. He took the fish to the tea table and let it slide on to the cake dish. It really looked most peculiar there, and it smelt a bit strong, too.

"Fish on dish. *That's* done," said Duffy, feeling pleased with himself. "Now then, where's my list again? I'm getting on famously. I've remembered the cake and the fish. What's the next thing?"

He read out his next entry. "Clock to go away. Dear me – *clock to go away!* Now, why in the world should the clock go away?"

He looked at the mantelpiece where the clock usually stood, but it wasn't there. Duffy frowned. Now where was the clock gone? He hunted around for it and at last found it standing by the kitchen door. He stared at it.

"Now what are you doing standing by the kitchen door, Clock?" he asked, puzzled. "You are usually on the mantelpiece. Are you ticking? No, you're not. You've stopped. You must be broken. Now why has Dumpy put you by the kitchen door? She usually puts things there when they are to go into the dustbin."

A thought struck him. "Oh yes – now I remember. Dumpy *did* say something about the dustbin. She must have asked me to throw the old broken clock into the dustbin! Well, come along, Clock, into the dustbin you go!"

Out he trotted with the kitchen clock, took off the dustbin lid and threw the clock in among the potato peelings and other rubbish.

He went back to the house. Paddy the cat was there, meowing loudly. She rubbed herself against Duffy's legs. "Oh, you've come back, have you?" said Duffy. "Where have you been?"

"Meeow," said the cat, and rubbed herself against Duffy's legs again, almost tripping him up.

"Now, wait a minute," said Duffy, pulling out his notebook again. "I seem to remember Dumpy saying something about you. Maybe you are the fourth thing I had to remember. Just let me look!"

He stared at the fourth thing he had written down. "Tea leaves. *Tea* leaves! – that seems a little peculiar. I'm sure I was to give the cat something to eat, but the only thing left to give it is tea leaves. At least, that's what I've written down. Well, Puss, I suppose it's all right. Maybe you like tea leaves. Cats are curious creatures!"

He found the tea leaves in the sink-basket and emptied them on to the cat's plate. Paddy sniffed at them in surprise. She gave them a small lick and then turned away in disgust.

"Well, well – you can't be very hungry," said Duffy. "Eat them when you feel like it! I'm going to sit down and have a snooze."

So he settled down in his armchair and shut his eyes. He was soon fast asleep. He didn't hear Dumpy come in with old Mrs Do-a-Lot. He didn't see her sniffing the air in surprise. What *was* that fishy smell?

"Oh, Dumpy, dear, do look – somebody has put a herring in your cake dish!" said Mrs Do-a-Lot, suddenly. "What a strange thing to do!"

"Well!" said Dumpy, in astonishment. "That's the herring I told Duffy to put on the cat's dish when she came

meowing for food. Duffy – DUFFY! Wake up at once,"

Duffy woke up. "Hello, Dumpy! How do you do, Mrs Do-a-Lot? I was just having a nap. Dumpy, I remembered to do *everything* you told me to!"

"Oh, *did* you?" said Dumpy. "Well, Duffy, will you please tell me why you put the cat's fish in the middle of the tea table? I didn't tell you to do *that*! Is it supposed to be a joke?"

"My notes said 'fish on dish'," said

Duffy, puzzled. "Look!"

"Duffy, what did you do with the *cake*?" asked Dumpy, looking all round. "I can't see it anywhere. It was the cake I wanted you to put on the cake dish. That's your first note, look, 'remember cake'. Where is it?"

"Oh, dear me – I thought the cake was for the messenger boy who called," said Duffy, shocked. "He said he had been told to collect something and I quite thought it was the cake. He seemed so delighted. He said his dad would be pleased too."

"His dad is the clock-mender, Mr Tick-Tock," said Dumpy, almost in tears. "I expect he *will* be pleased with my beautiful cake. I told you to give the kitchen clock to his boy – it's to be mended. Where's the clock, then?"

"Well, my dear – it was standing over there by the door – and I quite thought it was to go into the dustbin," said poor Duffy.

"You put my lovely kitchen clock into the dustbin! Oh, you wicked fellow!" cried Dumpy, and Mrs Do-a-Lot gave a loud snort of disgust. "I said you were to put the *tea leaves* into the dustbin. Where are your brains, Duffy? Oh dear, oh dear. And now I wonder what you did with the tea leaves?"

"He's put them into the cat's dish," said Mrs Do-a-Lot, with another snort. "Look! No wonder poor Paddy looks disgusted!"

"Well, there wasn't anything left on my notes to give her by the time she came meowing round," said Duffy, desperately. "It's her fault. If she had come right at the beginning of the afternoon I would have had the fish to give her. It's all her fault!"

"Why don't you put *him* into the dustbin?" said Mrs Do-a-Lot.

She looked so fierce that Duffy ran out of the kitchen door and locked himself into the wood shed. He was very sad. He had made all those notes – read them to himself – and had done a whole lot of things. But what was the use? They were all wrong!

Dumpy put her head in at the window. "Duffy, don't be silly. Come back. It's not the cat's fault and it isn't yours either, really. It's mine. I should have known that you would get it all wrong! And, by the way, Mrs Do-a-Lot says she knows why you are called Duffy."

"Oh, she does, does she?" said Duffy. "Well, why then?"

"Because it's short for Duffer!" said Dumpy, with a giggle. "I shan't call you Duffy again. Come on, Duffer, let's give Paddy her fish and then we can have some tea!"

Well, I can't help thinking Mrs Do-a-Lot is right. Poor old Duffer, he couldn't have made a worse muddle if he had tried, could he?

The marvellous pink vase

Once upon a time Mr and Mrs Squabble went to a fair. Mr Squabble spent ten pence on the hoopla, and tried to throw wooden rings over the things spread out on a table. Mrs Squabble spent five pence, and she was very lucky. One of her rings fell right over a marvellous pink vase.

It was very tall, and had pink roses painted all the way up. Mrs Squabble was simply delighted with it. When the man gave it to her she beamed with joy.

"Isn't it lovely?" she said to Mr Squabble as she carried it home. "I wonder where I'd better put it."

Now Mr Squabble only liked vases when they were put so high up on a shelf or bookcase that he couldn't knock them over. So he made up his mind that he would say the vase would look fine on the top of the grandfather clock.

When they got home Mrs Squabble put the pink vase down on the table and looked around her living room. "Now where shall I put it?" she said. "It must be some place where everyone will see it, because it really is beautiful."

"Well, my dear, I should put it on the top of the grandfather clock," said Mr Squabble at once.

"On the top of the *clock*!" said Mrs Squabble, in surprise. "What a silly place! You never put anything on top of grandfather clocks."

"Well, why not?" asked Mr Squabble. "It would be quite a new place. I should love to see it there. Then, whenever I looked to see the time, which I do quite twenty times a day, I should see the vase. It's a marvellous place."

"Well, I don't think so," said Mrs Squabble firmly. "I shall put it on this little table here, near your armchair."

Mr Squabble looked on in horror as he watched Mrs Squabble put the vase on a rickety little table near his chair. He knew quite well that the first time he reached out for his newspaper he would knock the vase over.

"Now, my dear," he said, "that's a foolish place. Only you would think of such a silly place."

"Oh! How dare you say a thing like that!" cried Mrs Squabble. "Just because I didn't like the top of the grandfather clock!"

"Well, if you don't like that, what about putting the vase safely up there on the top of the radio?" said Mr Squabble, trying to speak in a nice, peaceful voice.

"Really, Squabble, you do think of some stupid places!" said Mrs Squabble. "Why, every time you turned on the radio, the vase would shake and might fall over."

"I don't think so," said Mr Squabble.

141

"Though if you turn on the radio when that dreadful woman with the screeching voice sings, the vase might jump right off in alarm."

"I'll put the vase on the mantelpiece," said Mrs Squabble. But that didn't suit Mr Squabble at all.

"I shall knock it over when I reach up for my glasses," he said.

"Clumsy person!" said Mrs Squabble.

"Indeed I'm not!" said Mr Squabble. "Why, I could walk on flower pots all around the living room and not fall off once. And that's more than you could do!"

Well, of course, that was quite enough to make Mrs Squabble fetch in twenty flower pots from the shed and stand them around the living room.

"All right!" she said. "Now we'll just see who is clumsy and who is not! You start walking on the flower pots that side, and I'll start walking on them this side. And whoever falls off first has lost, and the other one can choose where to

put the pink vase. And let me tell you *this*, Squabble – that *I* shall win without any doubt at all!"

The two of them started to walk on the upturned flower pots. They did look silly. Round the living room they went, and round and round, neither of them falling off, for they were being very, very careful.

And then the cat jumped in at the window and made Mr and Mrs Squabble jump so much that they fell off their flower pots at the same moment and fell crash against the little table.

The pink vase was there. It wobbled – it fell over – it rolled off the table – it tumbled to the floor with a bang – and it smashed into a hundred pieces!

The cat sat in a corner and washed itself. "Now they'll both know where to put the marvellous pink vase!" the cat purred to itself. "There's only one place now – and that's the dustbin!"

Fly pie

There was once a big cat called Paddy. He was black and white, and had enormous whiskers. He was a great mouser – and sometimes he caught birds too.

But very soon the birds in the garden began to know Paddy, and to fly away as soon as he came near. The mice feared him, and ran to the fields. Even the rats wouldn't come into the garden. So Paddy couldn't chase anything at all.

He didn't really need to catch birds or mice, because his mistress fed him well. Three times a week she bought fish-scraps and boiled them for Paddy – and every day he had fresh milk and bacon rinds and scrapings of pudding, so he had plenty to eat.

But he loved chasing birds and mice. One day he sat in the garden looking up into the blue sky – and up there, flying high, he saw hundreds of birds! Far more than he ever saw in the garden, thought Paddy.

He sat and watched them. They were swallows with curved wings and forked tails. You can see them any day in the summer and early autumn, if you look up into the sky.

"If only I could get those birds down here!" thought Paddy. "Tails and whiskers, what fine fun I would have!"

He went to visit Kirry, the little pixie who lived under the hedge at the bottom of the garden.

"Kirry, what do those birds up in the sky eat?" he asked. "Do they nibble the clouds for their dinner – or eat a star or two?"

Kirry laughed loudly. "Those are swallows!" he said. "And they certainly don't eat the clouds or the stars – they catch flies all day long!"

"Oh, *flies!*" said Paddy, and he began to think. "Do they ever come down to earth, Kirry? There are such a lot of them up there."

"No – the swallows hardly ever come down to earth," said Kirry. "Only when they want mud for their nests, you know, and that's in the springtime."

"I wish I could get them down here," said Paddy. "I'd like to see them."

What he *really* meant was that he'd like to chase and catch them. But he didn't tell Kirry that, because Kirry loved the birds.

"Well – you won't get the swallows down here unless you give them as many flies as they can catch up there!" said Kirry.

"Oh," said Paddy, and he began to think hard. "Kirry," he said, "if I catch you a lot of flies, will you make me a fly pie, please? And send a message to the swallows to ask them to come down to tea here and eat the fly pie?"

"Well, that's very kind of you, Paddy," said Kirry, pleased. "Yes – I'll certainly make fly pie for you."

So for the next few days Paddy chased flies instead of mice or birds! There were a great many of the noisy bluebottles about just then, and many Daddy-longlegs, which the grown-ups hated because their grubs ate the roots of plants. So Paddy had a fine time chasing and catching these flies, and soon Kirry had enough to make a big fly pie for the swallows.

He sent a message to the birds. "Please come down to tea tomorrow. There is a big fly pie for you!"

The swallows twittered in the greatest excitement. "Fly pie! Fly pie! Did you hear that? We'll go and eat it, eat it, eat it! We'll go and eat it, eat it, eat it!"

So they sent a message back to Kirry. "Yes! We'll all come down tomorrow to eat your nice fly pie. Thank you very much!"

Kirry told Paddy. Paddy sharpened his claws and licked his lips. He would wait under the hedge for the swallows – and then spring out when they came, and catch dozens of them! What fun he would have! He looked at the fly pie which Kirry had baked. It looked fine, with a big crust on top, and a little pattern round the edge of the crust.

"They'll be here at four o'clock tomorrow," said Kirry. "Put a new bow of ribbon on, Paddy, and wash yourself well. It will be quite a party. It's so kind of you to think of fly pie for the swallows!"

Paddy grinned to himself. Yes, he had thought of a meal of fly pie for the swallows – but he had also thought of a meal of swallows for himself!

The next afternoon Paddy was well-hidden under the hedge. Kirry put out the fly pie, and put ready a little knife to cut it with. Now everything was ready. Only the guests had to come.

But they didn't come! No – not a swallow came! Kirry waited and waited – and Paddy hid and waited too. But no swallow flew down to the fly pie! Kirry looked up into the sky. It was quite empty of birds! Not a swallow darted in the air up there. It was very, very strange.

"Paddy!" called Kirry. "It's funny – but all the swallows have gone. I can't see a single one!"

Paddy came out, swinging his tail angrily. "*Gone!*" he said. "What do you mean, 'gone'? Just when I was looking forward to a good meal too!"

"A good meal?" said Kirry, astonished. "What do *you* mean? A good meal of what? I thought the fly pie was for the swallows!"

"A good meal of swallows, silly!" squealed Paddy, in a temper. "Are you so foolish that you didn't know that the

fly pie was only a trap to catch swallows for me?"

"Oh! You wicked cat!" cried Kirry. "No – I didn't know that at all, or I would never have made the fly pie for you! Now see what you have done! The swallows must have heard of your wicked idea – and they have all gone! Not one is left! Maybe they will never, never come back."

Paddy felt rather scared. Certainly the swallows had gone, there was no doubt about that – and how dreadful it would be if people got to know that he, Paddy, had driven them away because of his naughty idea!

Paddy began to slink away, ashamed of his trick. But Kirry was very angry and shouted after him:

"You're a bad cat! I don't want you for a friend any more! You and your fly pie! Here, take it – you're the only one likely to have it now!"

He threw the fly pie after Paddy. It landed on his head – and Paddy had to spend a most unpleasant half hour licking the fly pie off his thick black-and-white fur. Well, it served him right!

As for the swallows, they hadn't heard about the trap at all! You see, a cold wind had begun to blow the night before, and the chief of the swallows had decided that it was time to leave our country and fly to warmer countries far away!

So, with many twitterings, the swallows had gathered together, and then, with one accord, they had risen into the air and flown to the south! They would come back again in the spring – but Paddy didn't know that!

He just sat licking the unpleasant fly pie off his fur, thinking, "Well, never again will I try a trick like this! No, never again."

The riddling wizard

The riddling wizard wandered through the countryside, asking his odd riddles. If anyone could not answer, he made them pay him a golden piece.

So the country people were frightened when he came along, with his high pointed hat and his flowing cloak embroidered with shining suns, moons and stars.

He would stop on a village green, his big black cat beside him, and ring a loud bell. Everyone hurried to see what was the matter – and then the riddling wizard would get hold of someone and fire off his riddles.

They were always the same riddles, but no one could ever answer them.

In fact, no one believed they could be answered.

The first was this: "Pick up a stone from the ground. What tree will it grow into?"

The second was: "What creature has no wings and yet will fly through the air?"

The third was: "Bring me an apple that does not grow on an apple tree!"

As Jinky said, no one could answer riddles like that. "You can pick up as many stones as you like, but not one will ever grow into a tree! And how can anything fly if it has no wings? And who ever heard of an apple that did not grow on an apple tree?"

"It's an easy way for the riddling wizard to get money," grumbled Binny, the pixie. "He just asks his silly riddles and then fines us a gold piece!"

But after a while the riddling wizard got something more than a gold piece, as he wandered about. He made into servants all those who could not answer his riddles, and soon he had a train of miserable people following him, the black cat at the head.

Then the people of the countryside began to get really alarmed. They held a meeting. What were they to do about the riddling wizard?

"He's so powerful," said Kirry. "If we defy him, he will use his strong magic and turn us into hens that peck round his heels, or into snowflakes that melt in the sun, or mice for his black cat to hunt."

"What would happen if anyone answered his riddles?" asked Jiminy, a small goblin with a merry face.

"The person who can answer his riddles has the right also to ask the wizard three riddles," said Kirry. "He has said that if he cannot answer them, he will give his magic wand to his questioner. But that will never happen, because no one can answer his riddles, and certainly no one could ever ask him riddles he couldn't answer. He is very wise and very clever."

"Well, if he comes here *I* will try to answer his riddles, and ask him some of my own," said Jiminy boldly. The others stared at him.

"You are foolish," said Jinky. "You will have to pay him a gold piece – and you know you have only one, Jiminy – and you will have to follow him as his servant for the rest of your life!"

"All the same, I will try to answer his riddles!" said Jiminy. "So when he comes, let me know."

In two weeks' time there came word that the riddling wizard was coming to Jiminy's village. The people there were alarmed and excited. Jiminy was the only calm one.

"Don't be afraid," he said. "I will be the one to face him, so if anyone has to pay him and follow him it will be I, Jiminy, and not any of you!"

The riddling wizard came. He stood on the village green, with his large black cat blinking her green eyes beside

158

him. Behind him was his miserable train of servants, who were kept close to him by magic and could never run away.

The people came out of their houses. Jiminy was the first. It was he who faced the riddling wizard, and looked boldly at him. The wizard looked at Jiminy, and felt that it would be good to take money from this bold goblin and force him to wander behind him for miles.

"So you want to answer my riddles?" he said in his deep soft voice to Jiminy. "Then riddle me this! Pick up a stone from the ground. What tree will it grow into?"

Everyone watched Jiminy breathlessly. The goblin looked down on the ground, and then suddenly picked up something there. It was a cherry stone, dropped by someone who had sat on the green that morning, eating cherries!

"Here is a stone from the ground," said

Jiminy. "It will grow into a cherry tree!"

The wizard frowned. That was smart of Jiminy. Yes – it was a cherry stone – so certainly it could grow into a cherry tree, if it was planted. The wizard asked his next riddle.

"What creature has no wings and yet will fly through the air?"

Jiminy looked into a nearby bush, where he knew many caterpillars lived. He picked a caterpillar from the leaf it was eating and showed it to the wizard.

"Here is a creature that has no wings, and yet will fly – for it will change into a butterfly and wing its way through the air!"

Everyone clapped and cheered. How clever Jiminy was!

The wizard was not pleased, but he knew the answer was good. He asked the third riddle.

"Bring me an apple that does not grow on an apple tree!"

Jiminy crossed to an oak tree whose shady branches spread over the green.

He pulled a hard brown thing from a twig. It was an oak apple!

"Here is an apple that does not grow on an apple tree!" he cried, and threw the oak apple at the wizard in triumph. "Now I will riddle *you* three riddles! First, show me what goes as fast as the wind and yet makes no sound!"

"Easy!" cried the wizard, and before the astonished eyes of everyone he changed himself into a floating cloud, blown by the wind!

"Good!" cried Jiminy. "Now show me something so small I may hold it in my hand, and which yet contains something far bigger than I am!"

"Easy!" cried the wizard, and changed himself into an acorn which jumped into Jiminy's hand. Then, in a trice the wizard was himself again, and the acorn had vanished. "Was I not so small I was in your hand – and yet does not an acorn contain an oak tree?"

"Good," said Jiminy. "Now for my third riddle. Show me something that is often whipped hard and yet does no wrong!"

"Easy!" said the wizard, and changed himself into a pool of rich cream. Everyone stared and laughed. Yes, cream could be whipped, and yet did no wrong! Alas, the wizard had answered all the goblin's riddles.

Jiminy had guessed that the wizard would turn himself into a pool of cream. Quick as lightning the goblin called out to the wizard's big black cat. "Puss! There's your dinner!"

The black cat stared at the cream in surprise. She ran to it eagerly, and began to lap it up. A voice came from it.

"Stop! Stop! Let me change myself back to my own shape."

The cat took no notice. She lapped up all the cream, and then sat down and began to wash herself. Everyone stood silent for a moment. The wizard did not come back. He was gone. He had been licked up. Oh, clever Jiminy!

Everyone patted him and praised him, and the wizard's captives cheered and pranced about, for now they were free. Oh, clever Jiminy!

"You can have the wizard's wand!" they cried, and picked it up. "Then, if he manages to come back, he will be in your power."

The wizard never did come back, which was a good thing. The black cat settled down happily with Jiminy. Jiminy still has the wand, but he uses it for good magic and not for bad. He was clever, wasn't he? Could *you* have answered the wizard's riddles, do you think?

The enchanted gloves

Ho-Ho and Higgledy were two little brownies who lived in Sunflower Cottage on the edge of Honey Common. One was a painter and the other was a carpenter. Ho-Ho could paint a wall or a door in double-quick time, and Higgledy could make anything you pleased, from a giant's table to a canary's bath.

One day they had a message from Long-Beard the Chancellor of Fairyland. He lived in a palace nearby, and the two brownies often saw him out in his golden carriage.

Ho-Ho opened the letter, and read it out loud to Higgledy. This is what it said:

"The Chancellor would be glad if Ho-

Ho and Higgledy would call at his palace tomorrow morning to do some work."

"Ha!" said Higgledy, pleased. "That's fine! We shall get well paid for that! And it will be lovely to say that we work for the Chancellor. All our friends will know then that we are good workmen."

The next morning the brownies went to the palace. Long-Beard the Chancellor saw them, and told them that he wanted his dining room painted yellow and a new bookshelf made for his study.

165

"Very good, sir," said Ho-Ho and Higgledy. "We will start straight away."

They began their work, whistling merrily. Cinders, the Chancellor's black cat, and Snowie, his white dog, came to watch them. They sat solemnly there watching everything the brownies did.

"Do go away," said Ho-Ho at last. "You make us feel quite uncomfortable, staring all day like that."

"We like to watch you," said Cinders. "What a lovely colour that yellow is, Ho-Ho."

"I wish my tail was that colour," said Snowie the dog. "I hate being all white, and I think Snowie is such a silly name."

"Well, it's just as bad being all black," said Cinders. "It's very dull. Now if I were striped yellow I should feel grand."

"Will you have any paint left over when you have finished your job, Ho-Ho?" asked the dog.

"I might," said Ho-Ho. "But if you think I'm going to waste it on you, you're very much mistaken."

"Yes, but the Chancellor would be so pleased," said Cinders. "I'm sure he's tired of seeing us all one colour. He might pay you double for being so kind."

"I don't know about that," said Higgledy. "I've heard the Chancellor isn't very generous."

"Snowie! Cinders! Come and have your dinners!" called a voice. The two animals ran off and Ho-Ho and Higgledy went on with their work.

The next day and the next, Snowie and Cinders came and watched the two brownies. On the third day, when Ho-Ho had finished painting the walls a beautiful bright yellow and Higgledy had made a very nice bookcase, the two animals went over to the paint jar. They looked into it and then spoke to Ho-Ho.

"Ho-Ho, *do* let us have the little bit of paint that's left," begged Cinders. "We would be glad of it and we are sure the Chancellor would be pleased. Couldn't you just paint us yellow with your big brush? Do! Do!"

"Please!" said Snowie, wagging his tail hard. "How would you like to be dressed in nothing but white all your life long?"

"I shouldn't like it at all," said Ho-Ho. "But I don't know whether I dare do what you want."

The animals begged so hard that at last Ho-Ho and Higgledy gave in. Higgledy painted Snowie's long tail a most beautiful yellow, and gave him yellow ears too, and Ho-Ho painted long yellow stripes all down Cinders' black body.

They did look funny. Ho-Ho and Higgledy began to laugh when they saw how strange the two animals looked. But Cinders and Snowie were pleased. They ran out of the room and down the passage, and just round the corner they met the Chancellor.

He stared in astonishment and horror at his cat and dog. Whatever could have happened to them? Was this really Snowie, with yellow ears and tail?

What a horrible-looking animal! And could this really be his beautiful black cat, Cinders, with long yellow stripes all down his body?

"My eyes must be going wrong!" groaned the Chancellor. "Where are my glasses?"

He put them on and looked at the animals again – but they were still the same. What a terrible thing!

"Who has done this dreadful deed?" roared the Chancellor, suddenly feeling very angry. "Ho-Ho and Higgledy, is it you?"

He strode into the dining room and found the two brownies there, looking rather scared.

"How dare you paint my cat and dog!" shouted Long-Beard. "Get out of my palace at once!"

"But please, sir, Snowie and Cinders begged and begged us to," said Ho-Ho, trembling. "We didn't want to do it, but they said you would be pleased."

"I don't believe you!" said the

Chancellor, angrily. "You did it for a horrid joke. Go away at once and never come back!"

"We've finished our work," said Ho-Ho, "so we will go if you will kindly pay us, sir."

"Pay you!" cried the Chancellor. "Not a penny piece! Not a penny piece! Ho there, servants! Come and throw these wicked brownies out."

Two servants at once ran up, caught hold of the brownies, and threw them down the front steps of he palace. Ho-Ho and Higgledy picked themselves up and ran off in fright, leaving behind all their tools and brushes.

They didn't stop running till they came to Sunflower Cottage. Then they sat down in their little chairs and wept bitterly.

"Nasty, horrid old Chancellor!" said Ho-Ho. "We did our work. Why couldn't he have paid us? He just wanted to save the money, the mean old thing!"

"We'll pay him back somehow!" said

Higgledy, drying his eyes. "We'll go to Thumbs, the glove-maker. He's very clever, and perhaps he will think of some way to punish the mean Chancellor."

So next day they went to visit their friend, Thumbs. He made gloves – red ones, white ones, brown ones, blue ones, little and big, thin and thick. He was very clever indeed.

"Welcome!" he said, when he saw his two friends. He put down his work and set out three cups and three plates. "We will have some biscuits and cocoa. You look sad. Tell me your trouble."

So over their steaming cups of cocoa, Ho-Ho and Higgledy told Thumbs all about the mean Chancellor, and how he had thrown them out of the palace without paying them a penny just because they had been kind enough to do what Snowie and Cinders had begged them to do.

"We mean to punish the Chancellor, but we can't think how," said Higgledy.

"You are clever, Thumbs. Can you help us?"

Thumbs put his finger on his nose and rubbed it, thinking hard. Then he began to smile.

"I've got an idea!" he said. "It's old Long-Beard's birthday next week. I'll make him a pair of gloves and you can send them to him without saying where they come from. Inside the gloves I'll put a naughty spell. This spell will act as soon as he puts the gloves on."

"What will it do?" asked Ho-Ho in excitement.

"Why, it will make him pinch, punch and pull anybody who happens to be with him at the time!" said Thumbs. "Both his hands will act so strangely he won't know what is happening! They will pull people's noses, box their ears, tickle their ribs and pinch them! Goodness, how funny it would be to watch!"

Ho-Ho, Higgledy and Thumbs began to laugh till the tears ran down their noses and dropped into their cocoa. Oh, what a joke it would be!

All that week Thumbs worked at the gloves. They were beautiful, deep red with little yellow buttons and edged with white fur.

When the right day came Ho-Ho and Higgledy posted the parcel to Long-Beard. They decided to take a walk near the palace on the afternoon of the Chancellor's birthday, to see if they could hear what had happened.

Long-Beard had scores of parcels on his birthday. He opened them one after another, and most of them he didn't like a bit, for he was a mean old man. But when he came to the gloves – oh, my! What a fine surprise! What magnificent gloves! How warm! Who could have sent them? There was no card in the parcel and Long-Beard puzzled his head to think who could have given him such a nice present.

"It must be the King himself!" he thought at last. "He thinks a lot of me, and I expect he has sent me these gloves to show me how much he likes me. Well, I must wear them this afternoon, that's certain, for the King is calling for me in his carriage, and he will like to see his present on my hands."

So that afternoon, when the King's carriage rolled up at exactly three o'clock, the Chancellor stood ready. He carried his new gloves in his hand, intending to put them on as soon as he was in the carriage, so that the King would see them and perhaps say that he had sent them.

The King leaned out to greet his Chancellor.

"Come into the carriage, Long-Beard," he said. "It is a beautiful afternoon for a drive and we have a good deal of business to arrange."

Long-Beard stepped in and the door was closed. Just then up came Ho-Ho, Higgledy and Thumbs, out for a walk near the palace. Seeing the Chancellor getting into the King's carriage with the enchanted gloves in his hand they stood still in fright. Whatever would happen to the King when Long-Beard put on his gloves?

"Come on, we must go with the carriage!" cried Ho-Ho, and he ran after it. All three brownies swung themselves up on the ledge behind the carriage and sat there, unseen by anyone.

The Chancellor put on his gloves and the King looked at them.

"What beautiful gloves," he said – and then he gave a shout of surprise!

For Long-Beard's hands suddenly flew to the King's nose and pulled it hard! Then they went to the King's ribs and began to tickle him!

"Ooh!" cried the King. "Ooh! Stop it! Whatever is the matter with you, Long-Beard? Have you gone mad?"

The Chancellor was filled with horror. What was he doing? Why did his hands do such dreadful things? Why, they were boxing the King's ears now! He

tried to put them into his pockets, but he couldn't. They flew to the King's head, knocked his crown off and pulled his hair! Then they pinched his cheeks!

The King grew angry, and pinched the Chancellor back. Then he gave him a push that made the Chancellor gasp. The three brownies saw all that happened, for they were peeping in at the windows and they were horrified.

"Gloves, come to me!" cried Thumbs, suddenly.

At once the red gloves flew off Long-Beard's hands and went to Thumbs. The Chancellor's hands stopped behaving so strangely, and he stared at the King in shame.

The King stopped the carriage and got out.

"I must get to the bottom of this," he said. "What explanation have you, Long-Beard?"

"None, Your Majesty," said Long-Beard, trembling. "I don't know how it happened at all."

"Well, perhaps *you* can tell me the meaning of this!" said the King, turning suddenly to the three brownies, who stood nearby, red-faced and ashamed.

"Please, Your Majesty, I will confess everything," said Ho-Ho, and he told the King all that had happened – about the work done at Long-Beard's palace, the cat and the dog painted yellow, and the Chancellor's anger and meanness. Then he told how Thumbs had made the gloves to punish Long-Beard. The King looked stern.

"You had no right to think you could punish the Chancellor yourselves," he said. "You should have come to me and made your complaint. You have done wrong, and you must be punished. As for the Chancellor, he did wrong too, but he has been punished enough. He must certainly pay you what he owes you, but you must give half of it to the brownies' hospital. And you must polish my carriage until it sparkles."

So the three brownies had to spend all

day polishing the King's carriage. Then the King forgave them. The Chancellor opened his purse and with very bad grace gave Ho-Ho and Higgledy what he owed them.

"You might give me ten pounds to put in the hospital box too," said the King to the angry Chancellor. "I'm sure it wouldn't hurt you."

The three brownies walked home, not knowing whether to be glad or sorry.

"We'd better not be naughty any more," said Ho-Ho at last, "or listen to any more cats and dogs. What do you think, Higgledy and Thumbs?"

"We agree," said his friends. So for quite half a year they were as good as gold. And after that – ah, but that's another story!

A bit of luck for the goblin

There was once a goblin who thought himself very unlucky. He was always moaning and groaning about it.

"Do I ever have any luck?" he would say. "Do I ever find a spell anywhere? Do I ever have a nice bit of magic given to me? Do I ever have a wish sent me for my birthday? No, I never do!"

"Well, dear, never mind," said his wife, who got very tired of hearing the goblin grumble and grouse. "You've a nice little cottage and me for a wife, and two good suits of clothes, and . . ."

"Stop!" shouted the goblin. "Do you suppose that's all I want – a tiny cottage – only two suits of clothes –

and a garden that's always wanting to be dug – and . . ."

"Now, what's all this?" said a booming voice and who should pass but Mister Tricky. "Grumbling as usual about your luck, Goblin? Why, if you had a bit of luck you wouldn't know what to do with it! You'd lose it with your bad temper and grumbling!"

"I would not," cried the goblin. "I'd make the most of it! You should try me and see!"

"Right!" said Mister Tricky, and he took a belt from round his waist.

"Look, here's my wishing-belt. You can have it for a while. Take it in turns to wish, you and your wife. And mind you use this bit of luck properly!"

"Well!" said the goblin, and his wife gazed in delight at the red belt. The goblin took it. "This *is* a bit of luck!" he said. "I'll use it well, Mister Tricky."

"I'll come and get it back in a little while," said Tricky, and off he went.

The saucepan that was on the stove suddenly boiled over and the goblin's fat little wife gave a squeal. "Oh! The dinner will be spoilt. Give me the belt, quick, and I'll wish it all right again!"

She snatched the belt and wished for the dinner to be all right. The saucepan stopped boiling over at once. But the goblin was very angry. He grabbed the belt back.

"Fancy wasting a wish on your silly dinner!" he cried. "How dare you! We can wish for a splendid meal, silly! We don't need to worry about your stew! I wish for a roast duck and green peas!" he yelled.

At once a large dish of roast duck and green peas appeared on the table. "You're mean," said his wife. "You know I don't like roast duck. Greedy pig! Going to eat it all yourself, I suppose."

"Be polite to me," roared the goblin. "Get me a plate and a knife and fork."

The goblin's wife snatched up the red belt. "I wish the roast duck was on your head and the peas down your neck!" she shouted, angrily.

Well, the wish came true at once, of course, which was most unfortunate.

The duck leapt off the table and balanced itself on the goblin's head, with gravy dripping down his face. The peas emptied themselves cleverly down his neck. He gave a roar and grabbed the wishing-belt.

"You silly donkey!" he cried to his wife. "I wish you *were* a donkey! Then I could ride you to market and back and save my poor legs."

Well, his wife turned into a donkey, of course, and there she stood, pawing the floor and braying "*Hee-haw*" for all she was worth. The goblin stared in horror. He waved the belt in the air.

"I wish you weren't a donkey," he said in a trembling voice.

But nothing happened, of course, because it was his wife's turn to wish.

He put the belt on her back. "Wish yourself back to your own shape," he begged her.

The donkey hee-hawed her wish. But it wasn't to go back to her own shape. No – she meant to get her revenge on her unkind husband.

"I wish you were a carrot!" she brayed. "A nice juicy carrot. Then I could eat you!"

And the goblin changed into a carrot, of course. It was very awkward. He lay there on the floor, and the donkey moved up to him. She bared her teeth. The carrot trembled. The donkey licked him, and then did a gentle little nibble. The carrot squealed.

The donkey kicked the carrot out of the way, not really meaning to eat him. He fell on the wishing-belt and at once he wished very hard indeed.

"I wish I was myself, I wish I was myself!" And at once he was himself again, with the roast duck on his head and peas down his neck.

He put the wishing-belt rather humbly over the donkey's back. "Please wish yourself back, wife," he said. So she did, and there she stood before him, no longer a grey donkey but his fat little goblin wife.

"We've been silly," said the goblin, and he took up the wishing-belt. "I'd better wish away the duck from my head. It seems as if it's growing there for good!"

So he did – and the duck vanished, though the peas, which he had forgotten, were still down his neck.

"What a waste of a roast duck," said his wife, who was still angry at being turned into a donkey. She took the belt, and looked at the goblin. "I wish I had two nice fat cats of my own!" she said. And at once two big black cats came and sat by the fireside.

The goblin flew into a furious temper. "Haven't I told you I hate cats? Haven't I said I'll never have them in my house? I'll wish them away again!"

"Well, if you do I'll wish them back!" said his wife. "It'll be *my* wish next."

The goblin stopped just as he was about to wish the cats away. He had a much a better idea than that. He swung the belt and shouted: "I wish twenty dogs would come into the room! Then they'll chase out your cats!"

Well, no sooner had he wished than the wish came true, of course! Twenty dogs of all shapes and sizes rushed into the room. The cats at once jumped up the chimney! The dogs, sniffing the smell of the roast duck and gravy which hung about the goblin, turned to him and began to sniff at him and paw him.

The goblin's wife ran to pull them away. Then the dogs, thinking this was a fine game, began to chase the goblin and his wife round and round the kitchen. Oh, what a game they had! Over went the table and the chairs, and down went the dishes off the dresser!

"Get the wishing-belt quick, and wish!" yelled the goblin.

But one of the dogs had got it and was rushing out of the door to play with it!

And then, in the middle of all this, in came Mister Tricky, grinning from ear to ear. How he laughed when he saw the chasing dogs and the running goblins.

"Well, well – you seem to be in a bit of a muddle," he said. "Where's my wishing-belt? Ah, I see one of the dogs has got it. Here, boy, here! That's right, put it down! Well, well, Goblin, what a lot of dogs you seem to have got this morning!"

He buckled his belt round him and went to the door. "Hi, Mister Tricky!" cried the goblin, trying to push away a big dog. "Come back! Lend us your belt to wish these dogs away – and there's a couple of cats somewhere, and I've still got peas all down my neck!"

"Keep them!" said Mister Tricky, and walked off, laughing. "I want my belt now. Ah, what did I say to you, Goblin?

Didn't I tell you that if you did have a bit of luck, you wouldn't know what to do with it? I was right."

Poor goblins! They still have the dogs and the two cats, because they simply can't get rid of them. But it really was their own fault, wasn't it, for wasting some really marvellous luck!